THE CUCHARA
CHRONICLES

THE CUCHARA CHRONICLES

Tricia and Bob,
Happy reading!

Gary Bridges

Gary L. Bridges

Library of Congress Control Number: 2006903656
ISBN :   Hardcover   1-4257-1405-6
                  Softcover   1-4257-1404-8

To order additional copies of this book, contact:
Xlibris Corporation
1-888-795-4274
www.Xlibris.com
Orders@Xlibris.com
33574

CONTENTS

Dedication

To the memory of Leslie Hicks (1952-2004), cowgirl and friend,
so we may always see our past with affection.

I grew up dreamin' of bein' a cowboy,

And lovin' the cowboy ways.

Pursuin' the life of my high-ridin' heroes,

I burned up my childhood days. *

To my grandchildren, so we may always see our future with hope.

THE ARRIVAL

"This is not good," Lane Curry muttered silently as the Suburban's rear-end side-slipped on the snow-covered road. He eased off the gas pedal, and steered gently into the skid. The vehicle straightened itself, and Lane engaged four-wheel drive. When the indicator showed four-wheel engagement, Lane accelerated slowly. All four wheels were now holding traction on the fast-accumulating snow.

He had left San Antonio almost fifteen hours ago and was dead tired. Steve, his eleven-year old son, slept in the back seat. Passing through LaVeta, Colorado, Lane had begun to relax. There was no hint of snow, and their destination, Cuchara, was only eleven or twelve miles up the mountain on Highway 12.

The snowfall began almost as soon as he started the winding ascent and it become heavier and thicker as he inched his way up the mountain road. Lane was now straining to see the highway markers on the roadside. It had obviously been snowing for a long time, and no one had plowed the road. The white carpet grew thicker by the mile, muffling all highway sounds. Visibility was dangerously impaired by the surreal mix of darkness and swirling snow.

Lane sat forward in his seat, straining to see the road. He shifted into low four-wheel drive and slowed to a crawl. The outside thermometer glowed with the falling temperature: fifteen degrees . . . thirteen degrees. He realized he had not seen another vehicle since passing through LaVeta almost forty-five minutes ago.

About halfway up a particularly steep hill, the Suburban simply stopped. Lane couldn't believe it. The engine was running fine. He could feel all four tires spinning as he tried to accelerate. The wheels were turning, they just weren't going anywhere. The snow was too deep to negotiate and was turning the road into a giant slide. "My God!" Lane exclaimed out loud. Now he was slipping backward, down the steep hill, as gravity overcame his forward inertia. He couldn't see anything behind him. He remembered there was a wide ditch and a tall embankment on the right side of the road. He knew there was no guardrail on the left. It would be useless to brake. The best he could do was try to steer the rear end toward the right side of the road. An all-out backward spin would be disastrous. Lane turned the wheel as if he was backing down the hill under complete control. He felt the rear end turn and point in the direction he wanted. Suddenly, the lumbering Suburban came to a jolting but silent stop. The front end was cocked at an angle to the highway with the two front wheels turned at forty-five degrees and extruding out into the road. His headlights illuminated the tire tracks that were filling up with falling snow. Lane estimated twelve inches of snow on the roadway.

He must have backed into a snow bank, so there was no chance he would roll backward. Given the steep grade and the amount of snow, he was not going forward either. "Man, oh man." He sighed.

"Dad, where are we?" Steve asked sleepily. He crawled up from the back seat where he had been dozing peacefully since about Dalhart, just before they crossed the Texas border.

"I'm afraid we're stuck," Lane replied. "And I don't know how on earth we're gonna get out." Lane turned on his emergency flashers, opened his door to peer downhill, and gingerly stepped outside. The footing felt pretty solid under his left foot, so he stepped the rest of the way out of the vehicle and immediately fell flat on his back. Lane yelled the worst obscenity he knew.

"Dad, are you all right?" Steve yelled.

"Yeah, I'm okay." He rolled over and pushed himself up on all fours, grabbed the door handle, and slowly pulled himself up. It was certainly more dangerous outside than inside the vehicle.

Their options were as limited as they were obvious: stay put and wait for someone who could pull them out. He would leave the engine running to power the heater, and keep the headlights and the flashers operating. All of his friends had told him moving to Colorado was a really dumb thing to do.

"Steve, I think we're stuck here until someone comes along to help us."

"Okay." His response was muffled as he had already buried his head in his pillow.

"What a mess," Lane reflected. He had left Texas with such high hopes of reengineering his and Steve's lives. It had been almost a year since his wife had been killed in an auto accident. He and Steve had been trapped in a nightmare since then. Lane had decided the only way to break their cycle of grief was to move away from the familiar and start over. Lane had hoped to make this a place to start over. Now he just hoped to make it up the mountain.

Once he convinced himself there was nothing to do but wait, perhaps all night, Lane allowed himself to relax. He was determined to stay awake, though; it seemed to be his fatherly duty or perhaps his self-imposed punishment for getting himself and his son in such a predicament. His well-meaning and heroic resolve was useless against that most inexorable enemy of the vigilant—exhaustion.

It was hard to distinguish between dream worlds. The one he had just left, heavy with the silent whiteness of snow swirling in and out of the night's blackness, or the one he had just entered, following his wife into a darkening passage, calling her name with words that evaporated, like his breath in the cold Colorado air, as soon as he spoke. The louder he called, the faster she moved. He could always see her just ahead of him, but she would never turn around.

He *had* to ask her about their son Steve. Lane had always depended on her to act as chief communicator and translator between him and Steve. Not that he and Steve didn't communicate at all, but she was just so connected emotionally with Steve. She could read Lane's mind also, it seemed, in times of trouble or stress. Lane had been dependent on her insight, her understanding of both of them, and her endless compassion. She used to joke about taking care of both of her kids.

If he could just ask her what he should do now. What do I tell Steve about your death? How do I get him to talk about it? She just wouldn't turn around and look at him. If she would, he knew that she would stop and talk to him.

Lane jumped awake with a start. The snow-white world was bathed in brilliant light. Two giant roaring headlights were rushing down the highway straight for them.

Before Lane could decide what to do, the giant road plow came to a stop in front of him. The driver, bundled from head to toe, swung down from his enormous rig and came over to Lane's door.

"Where are you headed? Is everyone all right?" he yelled over the idling diesel engine.

"We're going to Cuchara. Anyway you can help us out?"

The driver was already removing a huge chain from behind the cab. Quickly, he squatted in front of the Suburban and attached it to the frame. He was under Lane's front end for less than thirty seconds. He jumped back into the cab and, with a nudge of a lever, raised the plow about six inches above the road. Now the chain was hooked onto the front end of the cab and snaked under the stranded Suburban.

"Cuchara is only two miles," he yelled over the engine. "There's not a good place for me to turn around for at least ten miles, so I'll just pull you in reverse. As soon as we get to the entrance of the village, I'll unhook you and you'll have it made. Just put her in neutral and steer lightly while I'm towing you."

Lane barely had time to get in and shift into neutral before they were moving up the highway in a surreal dance of lights and machinery. The plow's huge tire chains clattered noisily as they dug into the snow. Lane turned his headlights off but left his flashers on. The snow plow's rotating red beacon reminded him of an airport's rotating lantern. Large spotlights skewered the night from both sides of the cab. It was a smooth and effortless ride that brought them to the main (only) street in Cuchara. Lane got out and gingerly walked to the front where the driver was removing the tow chain from underneath his vehicle.

"I can't thank you enough. We were in a real jam."

"Glad to help. You'll have to wake up the hotel clerk. She sleeps in the room behind the desk. Just ring the bell until she hears ya. She'll be grumpy, but she'll be fine by mornin'. I've gotta run. Got a lot of highway to plow. Good luck." He was in the cab and moving the giant plow before Lane could speak. He looked at his watch. It was 2:30 a.m. He was sure his embarrassing arrival would be the topic of conversation among the villagers for days to come.

Finding their room and bedding down was uneventful. Both of them slept like the dead.

Steve was the first one to venture out in the morning. He was awestruck by the sight. Snow was everywhere! Their Suburban was covered by at least two inches. There must have been two feet of it on the ground. The pine tree branches sagged under the weight of their snow-covered needles. The extreme whiteness caused him to squint as the just-arriving sun made the snow glisten like tiny, scattered jewels. Downtown Cuchara appeared to be deserted. He turned toward the sound of a banging door. Someone had just walked into the Country Store. Steve wasn't sure how to navigate through the snow, so he just plowed through it, filling his boots with cold powder. The coldness assaulted his lungs when he inhaled and caused his exposed skin to ache. The door hinges whined, and a rusty bell tinkled when he walked into the store. The temperature change was almost stifling as the heat from a large black wood stove invited him to enter.

"Well, good morning." A booming, cheerful voice greeted him.

"Good morning," Steve replied as he looked around the decrepit but comfortable old building. The display cases were about half full and the aroma of fresh coffee filled the air. A couple of haphazard-looking old men sat at a card table right in front of the wood stove. A nondescript mutt raised his head and beat a halfhearted greeting on the wooden floor with his scraggly tail.

"You must be with the family who came in early this morning. My name's Missy and I'm the owner," Missy said as she stuck out her hand. Steve was immediately taken by her friendly nature and her engaging smile. He took her hand and remembered to look her in the eye as he returned the greeting. "My name's Steve Curry. My dad and I just got in, and I was wondering if there was any place we could get some breakfast." Missy gave his hand a squeeze before releasing it.

"LaVeta is the closest place for a hot breakfast this time of the year. Or you can heat some rolls in the microwave in the back over there to hold you over."

"Uh, okay. Can I just look around?"

Cuchara, Colorado Elevation 8,635

"Sure. Just be careful that Ben doesn't chew your leg off when you walk by." Hearing his name, the mutt raised his head as if to see what was required of him at such an early hour. Steve approached and Ben's tail tattooed a steady beat on the floor. Ben rolled over on his back and struck an inviting pose for a tummy scratch.

Steve desperately wanted his own dog. He bent down and rubbed Ben's belly. Ben rewarded him with a wet tongue on the chin. Steve remembered his mission—to find food. He walked around the aging store until he found prepackaged cinnamon rolls. Ignoring the vintage expiration date, he found the microwave and inserted them. While waiting for the buzzer, he poured a large cup of coffee and picked up a half pint of milk. Returning to the counter, he pulled dollar bills out of his pocket. He knew his dad would be surprised and pleased to have hot coffee greeting him first thing.

"You be sure and bring your dad over to meet everybody," Missy instructed as she packed Steve's purchase in a nice, tight box. She put a lid on the coffee cup and warned him not to take too long walking back or that coffee would be slush by the time he got to the hotel.

After dining on Steve's breakfast bounty, Lane and Steve dressed for their first day in Cuchara: both had long underwear, thick wool socks snugged down in insulated boots, and "gators"—waterproof leggings that covered the junction of jeans and boots and extended all the way up the shin to the knee. These kept snow from falling into the boots and kept the bottom of the pant legs dry.

Lane's reservations about moving were muted by the night's sleep and a growing sense of anticipation. They spent a leisurely morning meeting the few souls hanging around the Cuchara store, letting them know they were in the market for a rental house. Missy pointed out a few ragged For Rent notices on the bulletin board, none of which looked promising.

"Your best bet is to wait and talk to Jerry Anderson. He has more rental property under management than anyone else. Besides, he's the only one who comes into town this time of year," Missy said as she pointed to a small office next to the hotel entrance.

"Thanks. We might drive to LaVeta for a hot lunch if you think the road's safe."

"Oh, it'll be fine by now. Chris was out all night in the plow, and it stopped snowing about five," she replied. "Just don't get in a hurry."

His dad's driving lessons reverberated from years ago as Lane started toward LaVeta on the snow-crusted road. He slipped the automatic transmission into low gear. He wanted to avoid applying the brakes as they traveled down the curvy descending highway. By the time the road had leveled out, the morning sun had baked a good bit of the snow away, and it was clear sailing.

THE VALLEY

Cuchara is the Spanish word for "spoon" and, according to some of the longtime residents, refers to the spoon-shaped valley that meanders between LaVeta and Cuchara Pass along Highway 12, the "Highway of Legends." Early accounts show that the Native Americans called the valley Nunda Canyon, which means "Potato Canyon." Around the late 1800s, when the first Anglo homesteaders arrived to homestead on the free land, the scattered residents simply called their home Cuchara Valley. The soil and climate proved to be ideal for potato farming in the summer. Too good as it turned out, for the farmers wore out the soil and the potatoes shriveled up, as did the farmers' livelihood. Around 1910, the first resort community, Cuchara Camps, sprung up near the site of the current village. Ever since then, Cuchara has enjoyed, or endured, depending on whom you talk to, a robust summer tourist trade. Cuchara was now inhabited mostly by cattle ranchers, retirees, summer-time residents, a crippled ski resort, a growing golf course, and small businesses trying to eke out a living from the tourist trade.

Whether leading a wagon train of settlers west, traveling with a Comanche hunting party, or driving a bus full of skiers, one geographic certainty had loomed on the southern Colorado landscape, guiding adventurers or weary travelers, for hundreds of years—the Wahatoya. It meant "Breasts of the Earth," which were now referred to as the Spanish Peaks. These two prominent peaks defined southern Colorado and cast their shadows over the Cuchara Valley. The Mouache Ute, Comanche, Apache, Jicarilla, and other early Native American tribes crisscrossed the region using these peaks as their landmarks. Many of the tribes treated the peaks as sacred places. Other visitors included Spanish and French trappers, gold prospectors, hunters, American settlers, and conquistadors. There is evidence that the ancient Aztecs believed the peaks were laden with gold. Other travelers used names such as Twin Peaks, Dos Hermanos (Two Brothers), and the Mexican Mountains. But the name that stuck to the towering twosome was the Spanish Peaks. Separately, they are known as West Peak, the taller of the two at 13,626 feet, and East Peak, stretching to 12,686 feet, never quite matching its taller brother. In one respect, though, the peaks are even: they are clothed in magnificent layers of aspen trees, bristlecone pines, ponderosa pines, oak trees, and a dizzying array of colorful foliage. By late fall, the lower regions of both mountains are bathed in vibrant hues and capped off by crowns of fresh snow.

Spanish Peaks tower over the town of La Veta

Europeans traveling from Santa Fe first arrived at the Spanish Peaks in 1706, a good one hundred years before Zebulon Pike traveled up Pikes Peak. When the Santa Fe Trail was developed in 1821, the Spanish Peaks served as a landmark to travelers along the Mountain and Taos branches.

In 1862, Colonel John M. Francisco and Judge Henry Daigre established and manned Francisco Fort in the shadow of West Peak. These two intrepid frontiersmen and one Hiram Vasquez oversaw a large farming and ranching empire from this first settlement of the Cuchara Valley. Shortly thereafter, the story goes, the Ute chief, Ka-ni-ache attacked the settlement, driving all the inhabitants inside. Vasquez, himself raised by Native Americans, rode 120 miles to Ft. Lyon for help. By the time he returned with reinforcements, Francisco had negotiated a truce and avoided what might have been a bloody confrontation.

Soon, other settlers moved in to take advantage of the fort's protection and, by 1871, had established the area's first post office, aptly named Spanish Peaks. By 1876, the Denver and Rio Grande Railroad linked the growing community to the outside world. Soon thereafter, the post office was renamed LaVeta, which means "the vein" in Spanish.

In 1876, prospectors discovered silver lying within the peaks and soon were mining a series of shafts up and down the mountains. Remnants of the mining era can still be found today. One of the most accessible is Bullseye Mine, not far from the summit of West Peak. Halfhearted mining continued off and on until sometime in the 1940s and then was abandoned except for the occasional prospector with visions of lost Spanish gold or the mother lode.

Cuchara is sixteen miles south of LaVeta and heads a line of small remote mountain communities. Like sparkling beads splayed haphazardly along the shiny ribbon of Highway 12, Cuchara and ancient coal mining camps like Cokedale, Segundo, Madrid, and Valdez mark the way to Trinidad. Primero, Stonewall, Weston, and Tercio mark the beginnings of Bosque del Oso State Wildlife Area, one of America's prime elk habitats.

As dramatic as the Spanish Peaks are, lording over this gentle valley, as spectacular as is the vista of blue sky, reaching down to caress the foliage, and as grand as the Sangre de Cristo range looms, marching across the horizon, there are other unexpected geological features to astound and delight visitors—the Dikes.

The result of molten magma rising up through the earth's crust and seeping into vertical cracks and joints, the Dikes are a unique and defining feature of the Cuchara Valley. Erosion over millions of years has exposed these towering walls, some of which are one hundred feet wide and up to fourteen miles long. They radiate out from West Peak in all directions, like knobby points of a compass. Some are very distinctive and have been named by long ago, unknown residents. The Devil's Backbone, Profile Rock, and Stair Step all lie between LaVeta and Cuchara and provide spectacular viewing.

Lane had spent many of his boyhood summers in Cuchara visiting his great-grandfather. His great-great-grandfather, Sven Curry, had emigrated from Sweden and had built a house for his family not far from the Cucharas River. Two subsequent generations had added on to the original rock structure until it had become a comfortable two-bedroom house with running water and electricity. Lane's father tried to keep it up after *his* father (the last one to live there) died, but the distance and the elements worked against him. The house had been totally neglected since Lane's dad had died ten years ago.

Lane Curry was forty-five years old. If he had chosen a corporate career path, he would have been labeled a "fast burner" and would have been placed on the "fast track." He had an unquenchable thirst for knowledge. He was a learning junkie with a high-octane intellect. In college, professors had greatly admired him and wanted to tag along on his intellectual coattails or they had despised him because he was so alarmingly and obviously smarter than they were. With little effort, he had completed the requirements for the masters in business administration degree and the bachelor of sciences degree in four and a half years. A PhD in strategic management followed five years later. He began writing his dissertation at the end of the first year, much to the consternation of the faculty. After it had been accepted for publication and hailed as the academic "blockbuster" of the year, his dissertation committee came around and actually read it. He was the youngest faculty member ever awarded tenure at Texas's most prestigious college of business. The combination of a prodigious publishing record and a cultlike following of students had afforded him a near-legendary status on campus.

Lane's problem was that he got bored easily. He received a fellowship to study at Stanford for a year and stayed on to earn a PhD in political science primarily because he was fascinated with the cultivation and use of power. With an uncanny ability to synthesize large amounts of conflicting data, uncertainty, and ambiguity, Lane soon established a reputation for "forward strategic thinking." A reporter first applied the term to Lane's work in a *Fortune* magazine article. Lane had scoffed at the semantics because he couldn't imagine anyone being interested in *backward* strategic thinking. It just smacked of journalistic overhype.

His true love, it turned out, was studying and writing about the symbiotic relationship between corporations and politics and how that relationship influenced public policy at all levels. So many of the nation's strategic goals coincided with those of corporate America that it would seem only natural for the government and the corporate world to work together to forge public policy for the good of the country. What the taxpayers got instead was a fractious alliance between the country's rulers (legislators) and its distrustful warlords (corporate CEOs). The warlords squandered millions of their shareholders' dollars trying to influence policy while the rulers fought a perpetual war to hold or gain political territory at the warlords' expense.

A chance encounter with the owner of the Texas Rangers baseball team had launched Lane's lucrative consulting career. They had enjoyed a lively conversation about government intervention in the free markets vis-à-vis environmental regulations. It seems that the baseball magnate also ran the family oil and gas company. That family was politically connected, and the baseball heir soon launched his own political career. After he was elected governor of Texas, Lane had advised him on crafting legislation to protect the state's sensitive coastal areas without crippling offshore drilling. The legislation passed with the support of the oil and gas industry and was subsequently emulated by other states. A star, though reluctant, had been born.

Lane pulled into the off-street parking next to the West Peak Café in downtown LaVeta. He noticed the snow plow parked on the street. Crusty, dirty snow was melting from the undercarriage as the sun heated up the day. Steve and Lane discussed their housing search while they waited for lunch.

"Why don't we just live in Grandpa's house?" Steve asked.

"Well, maybe we will someday, but right now, it's not livable." What Lane left unsaid was that he wanted to be sure they were both going to be able to make the adjustment to living in a rural, mountain community before he made a major investment of time and money in the old family house.

Sights and sounds from the past flooded Lane's memory as he looked down LaVeta's main street. Charlie's Cash and Carry was the busiest place in town, as usual, with shoppers wandering in and out, trading news of the day, stories about the weather, and collecting their groceries. Charlie's defined the center of LaVeta socially, economically, and geographically.

LaVeta's high school, middle school, and elementary school occupied two buildings (including the gym) two blocks away. Basketball and volleyball fans were greeted by a ten-foot-high mural of an Indian in a war bonnet dunking a basketball. Lane smiled as he remembered the local reaction when an out-of-state activist righteously demanded that LaVeta change the mascot from the Redskins to something more politically correct. Suffice it to say that the activist was glad to escape with his scalp intact.

They found a house to rent on the third day of looking. The log cabin sat on a secluded lot about a mile from the base of the ski resort, huddled in a mixed grove of aspen, ponderosa pine, and blue cedar trees. A rutted driveway carved its way through the aspen trees to the front porch. It faced south, so the front windows received sunlight almost all day as did the driveway. The wooded, snow-draped backyard bore testimony to its perpetual shady condition. There were no other homes in sight. The Cuchara Ski Resort developer had encountered obstacles to financing the residential master plan and had stopped building after only one house.

The interior was spacious and drenched in midday sunlight. The furniture was comfortable but sparse. A rock fireplace with a rough-cut cedar mantle dominated the living area, which shared space with a small, neat kitchen. Plate glass windows provided a 270-degree view. The back of the tree-covered lot sloped slightly downhill for about one hundred feet then leveled out into a large open meadow.

The cabin's owner was locked in heated negotiations with the ski resort over the possible sale of the cabin and was happy to earn some rental income in the meantime. He had been one of the original owners of the ski resort but had sold his share about four owners ago. The cabin and its ten acres were his last pieces of property, and they stood right in the middle of the proposed residential development. Lane understood that if it sold, they might have to move on short notice. Given that it was intended for eventual development, the resort management maintained the gravel road and kept it plowed during the winter months so potential buyers could more easily shop for high-priced lots.

It took a couple of days to get the utilities turned on. By then, Lane and Steve were tired of the hotel room and anxious for some physical activity. They started early one morning. Lane carried in firewood from the backyard and soon had a roaring fire in the old fashioned wood stove. Steve found a snow shovel in the garage and began clearing the driveway. They cleaned in a steady frenzy all day, anxious to get settled.

The ski resort had proven to be a schizophrenic economic development project for the Cuchara Valley. Beset by chronic financial woes, undercapitalization, finicky winter temperatures, unreliable snow, and winds that some said could scour the bark from a tree, the resort had limped along for ten years. Owner after owner had poured millions into the resort and had helplessly watched their cash melt away as quickly as April's muddy snow.

Geographically, Cuchara was an ideal location to serve the ski-starved families from Texas, Oklahoma, and Kansas. Most of them could reach Cuchara in one day without crossing a difficult Colorado pass. However, there were never enough overnight accommodations for Cuchara to be considered a destination resort. Colorado front range skiers had too many other skiing options and did not consider Cuchara to be a serious ski resort because there were not enough expert ski runs to entice them. Because of its limited terrain and unpredictable snow, Cuchara could not charge the higher lift ticket prices needed to sustain operations.

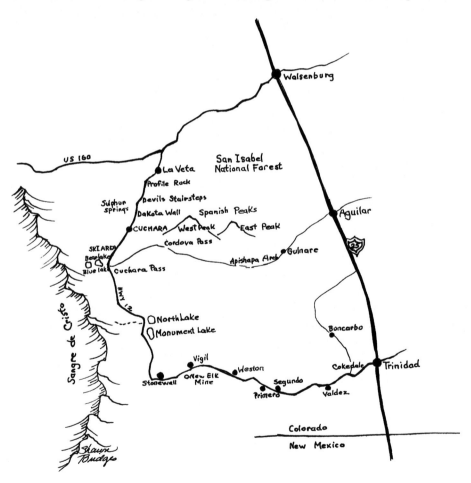

Map of State Highway 12
"The Highway of Legends"

Ski resorts, by nature, are burdened with high overhead costs and a slew of fixed costs. Snowmaking (a necessity at Cuchara) was extremely expensive. Water was fed up the ski slopes by electric pumps, mixed with enzymes, then pumped through hoses to all parts of the mountain and blown through fans into the freezing atmosphere where it was magically transformed into snow. On good days in Cuchara, the manmade snow supplemented the natural snow. On bad days, manmade snow was all they got. On really bad days, the temperature and the wind worked together in a devilish plot to melt it all into slush or to scour it into an icy glaze. The mountain manager often spent all night with the snow cat drivers trying to groom the slopes with quickly diminishing snow.

Chris Boone was the first visitor to the Curry household. The frozen ruts of the dirt and gravel driveway rattled his aging and permanently dirty pickup. It was a gray, cold Friday morning in March. He found Steve carrying a load of firewood onto the front porch.

"You're Steve, aren't you?" Chris offered his hand as Steve stacked his armload of aspen onto a growing pile.

"Yes, sir." Steve took Chris's hand and squeezed it firmly as he shook it. His eyes never left Chris's face. "Glad to meet you. I'm sorry my dad's not home right now. Can I help you?"

"Naw, I don't need anything. I just wanted to say hello. I heard you'd moved into the cabin. I'm Chris Boone. I pulled you and your Dad up the mountain your first night in town. Quite a welcome, huh?" Chris flashed a huge smile as he slapped Steve on the back.

"Oh, wow! What a cool truck! Can I ride in it sometime?" Steve had always loved big machinery—the louder, the better. A monster truck with big lights, huge tires, a steel plow, and tire chains fit his criteria of extra cool.

"Are you kiddin'? I'll teach you to drive it. In fact, after our next big dump, I'll pick you up down at the highway and you can make the rounds with me. Where's your dad?" Chris surveyed the tidy front porch.

"He drove to Pueblo to talk to someone at the university about a job. He said he would be back by dark."

As in most small rural communities, news of strangers raced feverishly through the gossip network. Chris had heard all the scuttlebutt about the widower from Texas and his shy youngster. The Curry family had been one of the early settlers of the valley. Lane's grandfather had mysteriously disappeared and presumably died, a result, some of the old-timers said, of the gold rumored to be hidden on his property. The family still owned almost two hundred acres that straddled the Cucharas River and cradled the family homestead. Lane's father had used the hundred-year-old rock house mainly as a hunting lodge and summer vacation haven. As he aged, the family had used the house less and less, and it had sagged into disrepair.

Chris smiled at Steve as he recognized something in his manner, or maybe it was the tilt of his head or his sincere gaze.

"Did you know that your dad and I were buddies many years ago when his family spent the summers here?"

"No. Really?" Steve was taken aback. He had never known anyone who knew his dad as a young boy. Steve's grandfather had died when Steve was just a baby, so he had never known him.

"I didn't recognize him that first night, but once I heard who you were, I made the family connection. The Boones were good friends of the Curry family, and my grandfather and your grandfather got to be real close. They used to hunt together and always talked about finding gold," Chris explained.

"Did you know my grandpa? I don't remember him at all," Steve once again probed his memory for a glimpse of his grandfather to no avail.

"Yes, I did. He was a very quiet and kind gentleman who always said hello to me. He was always helping folks and was good to all his neighbors. He was a hard worker and usually had cattle on the property. He also had a Border collie named Jumper who helped him with the cattle."

Steve was mesmerized. He had never heard stories like this. The look on his face encouraged Chris to continue.

"The last summer your dad spent here, he became my idol. He was eighteen or so and I was about eight. I remember he was a senior in high school and was always working out to get in shape for football practice. Even though he was much older, he always let me and a few other kids hang around with him."

"They won the state championship his senior year, and my dad was All State," Steve interjected. His mom had shown him the scrapbook full of clippings.

Chris continued, "Well, I'm not surprised. He was strong as an ox and could run all day." Steve saw Chris's eyes dancing as a big smile broke out across his face. Chris actually laughed out loud. "Man, oh man. I had completely forgotten about that day on Three Sisters until this very minute.

"Your dad used to go running on the trail that zigzagged around the Three Sisters." Chris could see the puzzled look on Steve's face. "Come over here," he said as he pulled Steve along the driveway and pointed east. "Notice those three small round peaks? They're tiny compared to West Peak and East Peak. Well, those are North White Peak on the left, Middle White Peak in the middle, and South White Peak: the Three Sisters. There's a trail that wanders all around in there and takes you along the crest of a couple of the Sisters. It was in June . . ."

THE THREE SISTERS

Lane was as relaxed as a human body could be and still be upright and moving. It was a typical summer day in Cuchara. The sky was so blue it almost hurt your eyes. The morning chill lingered as the sun struggled to invade the shadows, and Lane moved silently among the ponderosa pines and aspens. He loved running on the Cottonwood Canyon Trail; Lane's breathing was almost in perfect sync with his legs as he glided over the steeping trail on his morning run.

Through this perfect harmony of nature and spirit peeked a tiny but growing disharmony—a cry or a wail that jarred Lane and caused him to slow down to listen. It was plaintive, painful, and pitiful. He stopped to orient the sound to his position. A discordant bawling sent shivers through him. What in the world? Almost childlike, it was unmistakably a cry of distress and suffering. Lane resumed his running but frantically now as his legs carried him closer to the sound.

The trail blossomed out into a clearing, and Lane drew up sharply, unable to take in the scene and all the participants. Chris Boone turned to look at him, holding his little sister's hand, which was sidled up to him so tightly they were probably just making one shadow.

The object of their obvious consternation and the source of the wailing stopped Lane cold. It was a bear cub. Its size told Lane that it was less than a year old, which meant it had been born this past winter during the sow's hibernation and had only been out of the den since about March or April. Lane was horrified. The cub was tied to a tree, an old dirty rope around its neck. It writhed and pulled on the rope as it spun round and round in one spot trying and trying to free itself. Exhausted and frightened, the cub's wailing had turned into a pitiful whimper.

Lane looked at Chris and saw the fear in his eyes. Lane could see he was barely holding it together as he tried to comfort Jenny and protect her. Protect her from what? The laughter finally registered with Lane. Three rambunctious young men were taunting the cub, poking at it with sticks, front and back, as the cub cowered and pulled at its tether.

Lane recognized the three. They were guests of the Burchfields, first-time guests who had not distinguished themselves with their manners. They already had a brush with the local law over drunkenness and fighting with some of the locals. Lane also knew that one of them, Duncan Weaver, was the next starting inside linebacker for Penn State. He had been the Nittany Lions' leading tackler this past season.

Lane ignored the three and walked straight toward the tree to untie the cub. He was airborne by the time he felt all the air in his lungs rush out with a mighty whoosh as his left rib cage folded in. Years of football practice and thousands of tackling drills had trained Lane's body, and the second before he exploded onto the ground, his right shoulder rolled under him. His momentum carried him through the roll, and he was on his feet in one fluid movement. His ribs were just now feeling the sharp pain from the tackler's well-placed shoulder. Lane quickly assessed his situation—he could probably do some serious damage to the grinning face closest to him. He imagined his fist smashing into Duncan's nose, sending blood, snot, and crushed cartilage flying everywhere. But he knew that was foolish. He was outnumbered three to one. He also had Chris and Jenny to think about . . . and the bear cub. Lane's emotions shifted gears as he stepped forward.

"Hey, guys, I'm sorry. I didn't mean to interfere with your fun here," he said as he waved toward the struggling cub. "But I just don't want to get in trouble with the local game warden. He's bound to get a call from someone since I could hear this guy bawling all the way down at the trail head," Lane exaggerated. *Ahah, I've got them*, Lane thought as he noticed just a split second of doubt rush in through all the testosterone.

The biggest one, Duncan Weaver, stepped forward. "What do you mean?"

"Well, this summer, the bear problem has been especially severe due to the dry winter and spring up here. That means there isn't enough food for the bears in their normal feeding grounds up higher, so they wander around the campgrounds and even in Cuchara to forage for trash. The game warden, Ronnie Evans, is constantly answering calls from the cabin owners and businesses to do something. All he can do is put out live traps, you know those bright green, metal cylinders on wheels, and transport the trapped bears out of the area. He puts a tag in a bear's ear the first time he traps it. If that same bear has to be trapped again or even shows up getting in someone's trash, Ronnie has to shoot it. And that makes him very cranky," Lane explained. He went on, "Most tourists who haven't been in Colorado very long don't understand how much authority the game wardens have. They have jurisdiction just about everywhere and anywhere they think they need it. The local law and the local judges rely on the game wardens to support the local law enforcement efforts, so they always support the game wardens. I just don't want to be around when he comes to investigate this distress call," Lane said soberly.

The three traded glances. Duncan spoke again, "Okay, what would you do?"

"I would untie this guy and have Chris here carry him away from here. He knows how to handle him." Lane shot a look at Chris who nodded and then replied, "Sure, Lane, I'll take care of it."

"Well, we don't care what you do. Just get him out of here," Duncan snarled.

Lane turned and slowly walked toward the cub. The little guy was exhausted and couldn't put up even a show of bravado. Lane grabbed the rope and slid his hands down to the cub's neck and began to untie it. He got blood on his hands from the underside of the rope as he removed it from around the cub's matted neck.

Rage welled up just below his calm demeanor. The cub weighed about thirty-five pounds. He carried it to Chris. "Can you get him down the mountain all right?"

"Sure, I can do that." Chris cradled the young bear.

"I'll call you later. You know what to do."

Lane was also worried about the cub's mother. Normally, she would have come running if she heard one of her cubs carrying on. She had either been killed by an illegal hunter, had starved to death, or was trapped in one of the live traps. The little cub's chances of survival were not good, especially given the trauma it had just suffered.

Black Bear (Ursus americanus)

Lane was seething. Cruelty to animals was unforgivable in his eyes, and to frighten and embarrass Chris in the process . . . Lane pulled out his most formidable weapon.

"Say, you're Duncan Weaver, aren't you?" He held out his hand to shake. Duncan looked surprised.

"How do you know my name?" He looked both surprised and smug.

"Heck, if you read *Sports Illustrated*, you can't *not* know Duncan Weaver. Preseason consensus All American, leading tackler on the best Penn State team in history, and early favorite to win the Outland Trophy next year," Lane gushed. "We're honored to have you here." Lane's calm demeanor belied his devious plotting.

"So are y'all going to be here for the Fourth of July parade?"

"Yeah, we're gonna be here. Why, do you ride a tricycle in the parade?" Duncan snorted and then laughed coarsely. Lane smiled, thinking, "Oh no, I've got something much better in mind."

"Listen, I play football too. In Texas. Why don't we stage a July 4th challenge to climb West Peak? You know, kind of like a fun run? I've been up there a couple of times. It only takes a couple of hours to get to the top. We could be back down well before the parade. What do you say?" Lane was betting on an emotional acceptance without having to answer very many technical questions about the nature of this "climb."

Duncan wondered if he was in danger of being conned, but his brain had a hard time holding any one thought very long, and the caution flitted away. This was a physical challenge. His "me big-me strong" genes kicked in and drowned out his "be careful" genes with hard-rushing adrenalin and he blindly accepted.

The entire Cuchara Valley was soon buzzing with excitement. Even though Lane was not a true Cuchara local, his family history in the valley and his personality granted him "almost local" status. Plus the story of the encounter on Three Sisters became well known. The Fourth of July was two weeks away, and the local newspaper, the *Valley View*, got hooked on the celebrity status of Duncan. A stringer for the *Pueblo Chieftain* who lived in LaVeta called her friend at the *Denver Post*. The *Sports Illustrated* columnist Rick Reilly lived in Denver and interviewed both Lane and Duncan on the telephone. The excitement was building.

A small group of local climbers considered themselves the unofficial guardians and overseers of West Peak (they called themselves the "At Our Peak" club) and offered to officiate the event. One of them would climb the peak before the race and place a small flag at the top. The first contestant up the peak would bring it down. Since only the club members would know ahead of time what the flag looked like, nobody could cheat. Pete Robbins, the local US forest ranger would serve as the official starter.

The tourists and summer residents were soon bombarded with all the truths, myths, mysteries, and legends of West Peak and the smaller brother East Peak. The stories flew about the various airplane crashes that had left pieces of wings and who-knows-what-else on the mountains. Todd Lincoln, son of Abraham Lincoln, had been a part owner of the Bulls Eye mine, nestled on the other side of West Peak. Climatological lore was a favorite. West Peak, at 13, 626 feet, could be deadly to those who got caught in the open during a thunderstorm. Lightning had struck Ben Livingston in 1952 and fried both his testicles.

It was imperative that climbers get down before noon. Casual hikers often ended up seriously ill from altitude sickness.

What no one bothered to tell Duncan was that Lane had been running up West Peak three times a week since early June as part of his conditioning regimen. Lane had told LaVeta's football coach that he wanted to be the best conditioned athlete in Texas when his high school's two-a-day workouts started. They were expected to make a run for the Texas state championship, and Lane also knew that the college scouts would be watching closely. He used LaVeta's weight room three or four times a week. He was certainly the best conditioned athlete in Cuchara that summer, as the Penn State Nittany Lions would soon find out.

The race would begin at sunrise. The Cuchara Ski Resort was advertising a sunrise breakfast on the Baker Creek restaurant deck. They had bought fifteen telescopes for guests to rent and watch the whole spectacle.

Lane was confident he would beat Duncan to the peak. Not only was his conditioning superior, he knew that no one could last physically at that altitude after only a few days of acclimation. The trek to West Peak was not technically a climb but a steep hike. There was certainly no need for climbing gear. The footing could be treacherous as the "path" (there was not technically a trail once you left tree line) was covered in loose rocks.

The West Peak trail meandered from the parking lot at Cordova Pass, with an eleven thousand feet elevation, to tree line (the point beyond which no trees grew). Lane also wanted to work on Duncan's mind a little bit, so he spent the night in his sleeping bag at tree line and was drinking hot tea when they arrived. He had also been drinking water constantly since dehydration could pose a real danger. The West Peak Trail was a gentle but steady ascent punctuated with sharp turns and required scrambling over the occasional fallen tree. Duncan was flushed from the exertion and was breathing heavily. He sat down to rest. The Cuchara Rescue Squad had sent EMTs to stand by at the starting point. They laid it on pretty thick for Duncan's benefit. Nobody was immune from the atmosphere of "locals vs. outsiders" that pervaded the valley.

Jimmie Cook, the paramedic, addressed both of them. "Remember that thunderstorms can come up very quickly and without warning. If you feel the hair on your neck or your scalp starting to stand up, immediately squat down, wrap your arms around your knees, and balance on the balls of your feet. This will present a much smaller target for lightning strikes. Don't forget to drink plenty of water. Dehydration can cause extreme disorientation. If you fall and break a leg on the mountain, it could take us hours to get you down. Good luck to both of you."

A small group of hardcore *At Our Peak* enthusiasts had gathered to stand watch during the race. Duncan's two buddies seemed to sense the overwhelming support for Lane. They both showed looks of discomfort and spoke only to Duncan or to each other. Dawn crept through the shadows and chased the darkness away. As soon as they could see more than dark outlines, Lane and Duncan began the first annual Fourth of July race to the peak.

Normally Lane began his West Peak workouts with a steady but brisk walk to allow his cardio system time to speed up gradually, but he wanted to demoralize Duncan early, so he took off in a jog. After fifteen minutes, his walk slowed to fast long strides. He hiked swiftly and resolutely for fifteen more minutes before taking time to stop and look back. Duncan was already struggling. Lane pushed on, anxious to widen the gap.

Duncan's lungs burned. He labored to get air, and each breath left his body screaming for more. His knees trembled. Not only did he have to hike at a ridiculous angle, but his feet were constantly sliding with the loose rocks. He fought to keep his balance, expending even more precious energy. He began to feel lightheaded from oxygen deprivation. His brain, overtaxed in the best of circumstances, struggled to maintain focus. No matter how often he stopped to catch his breath, he could never get enough. He wanted to quit but didn't know how.

Lane usually made it to the top in less than two hours. He guessed that today's time would be around one hour and forty-five minutes or less. He drank a long drink and resumed his upward hike, picking up speed again. He wanted to pass Duncan on his way down, before the big buffoon had to be carried off the mountain. Lane knew that Duncan's weight, oxygen deprivation, and his flatlander legs would keep him from the top. Lane smiled to himself. The best part was what Duncan did not even know yet. Getting down was even more strenuous than getting up. His knees and thighs would scream when Duncan tried to brake himself on the steep descent.

Lane reached the summit in one hour and forty minutes. He allowed himself a few minutes to breathe deeply and drink water. As always, the view from West Peak was stunning. The 360-degree panorama never failed to overwhelm him. It was truly a symphony for the soul: the largest palette in the world with the dark greens of ponderosas and the shimmering lightness of aspens accenting the whiteness of winter's snow still trapped on the neighborhood peaks. Trinchera Peak stood sentinel to the southwest and Mount Blanca to the northwest. Lane allowed himself a few quiet moments before getting back to business. He found the winner's flag, tucked it into his belt, and started home.

He had perfected his descent technique by now and virtually ran down the mountain side. He constantly adjusted the angle of his body to the mountain as he looked ahead to pick the best route.

By the time Lane got almost to tree line, he could see Jimmie holding a bag of fluid up in the air. The experienced mountain rescue guide had had to climb up the mountain's slope to administer an IV to Duncan when he collapsed about halfway up. He was dangerously dehydrated. With help from Jimmie and an EMT, Duncan stumbled back down the mountain side. They managed to get Duncan back to the parking lot and loaded him up in the rescue truck. They rushed him to the hospital in Walsenburg, where he briefly lapsed into unconsciousness. After a night of IVs, Duncan fully recovered. His buddies were scared and morose. They left Colorado the next day and were never seen again.

"Well, I gotta go. Tell your dad I came by. I'll catch him later." Chris waved and was soon backing out of the driveway.

A NEW HOME

Lane accelerated quickly to merge with the southbound traffic on I-25. His meeting with the president had gone extremely well. Blaine Rutherford had been president of State University for almost a year now. He had taken the job in the midst of the most extraordinary university restructuring in anyone's memory. Blaine had been provost of Stanford University for five years and had been Lane's advisor and mentor during his PhD program. "Small world, I guess," mused Lane as he left Pueblo's city limits and headed to Cuchara.

State University was both a gem and a thorn to the Colorado State Legislature and the governor. Several coeds had accused SU football players of raping them. The rapes had allegedly occurred as a result of assistant coaches arranging sex for high school football recruits. The athletic director had resigned under a torrent of blistering media coverage. The head football coach had refused to acknowledge any responsibility for the actions of his assistant coaches or players. The president of the university resigned amidst the grand jury investigation and thumbed her nose at the board of regents and the legislature on her way out. Before the acrimony from this debacle had a chance to cool down, an SU professor published a manifesto accusing American citizens of war crimes for supporting the war in Iraq and claiming Osama Bin Laden was a hero and that the United States deserved all terrorist acts committed against its citizens. The professor was tenured and Hispanic (or so he claimed). It turned out there was considerable doubt about his heritage, and he seemed to have been very lax about properly and completely attributing many of the sources he used for a variety of his past publications. Bill O'Reilly had a field day in his "No Spin Zone," and the public outcry against the professor's hate mongering struck an angry chord with the state legislature, especially when it was revealed that SU's tenure process had been bent so far out of shape for him that it was unrecognizable. Many legislators had, at various times, been embarrassed and even ridiculed by SU presidents. Even the historical and sometimes hysterical SU supporters fell silent under the crescendo of public anger at the anti-American ranting of SU's vocal faculty who dared them to fire one of their own. They wrapped themselves in the mythical cloak of academic freedom and virtually taunted the governor. But enough was enough. The governor and a few key legislators set out to do the unthinkable. They gutted SU's budget, but with a sardonic twist. They would restore funding to those departments that relocated to Pueblo, home of Southern Colorado University, a small regional university under the same governing body. The legislature funded $50 million in new construction for the Pueblo campus. The city council and the mayor of Boulder, home to the incredibly shrinking SU, as well as the SU faculty shrieked their indignation. Boulder's elites and intellectuals mustered formidable legal and political firepower to counter the so-called rape of their beloved university. They had trampled the legislature's dignity once too often though. A flood of legislation and budget amendments drowned out the protestations. The "new SU" had been born, and Pueblo was the proud mother.

Blaine Rutherford was the perfect president for the "new SU." He had cut his academic molars at Berkeley, was a distinguished scholar—a near genius, who looked like the Hollywood prototype star quarterback, an eloquent quarterback with a scathing wit. He had been the only faculty member at Stanford who had intellectually challenged Lane. The thought of working with him again ignited a flame that Lane thought was snuffed out forever when his wife, Becky, died. Lane had to admit that he missed the students. He missed being part of their learning process, seeing that spark of understanding and excitement. Maybe this move was going to work out.

Even with prodigious amounts of money pouring into the Pueblo campus, it had proved difficult to attract big-name faculty. Blaine told him they were about 20 percent behind their hiring goals across all disciplines. Lane would be welcomed because he could fill a position in the college of business that was desperately working for their first accreditation. Lane's credentials would sit well with the accreditors. He would develop and teach one MBA course, *Strategic Management: Entrepreneur to CEO.* He would also develop Executive MBA seminars on *political power and corporate governance.* The idea was to develop a center for responsible and responsive corporate governance at SU. Through years of gritty and dogged economic development efforts, Pueblo had assembled a rather impressive array of Fortune 1000 corporations in and around the city. Many of their midlevel managers attended MBA classes at SU. Their senior executives were the target market for the seminars. Lane would teach at least five seminars a year, traveling to Denver and other points to attract a following. His list of publications and his occasional stint with Tim Russert would help generate audiences.

SU would pay him just a smidgen over $110,000 for a nine-month contract, and he would get 50 percent of the outrageous fees to be charged for his seminars. He and Blaine had agreed that he would work as a nontenure track faculty. SU was the first research institution to embrace and actually hire experienced faculty as nontenure track. Existing tenured SU faculty who moved to Pueblo kept their tenure, but all new faculty members were being hired as nontenure track because Blaine Rutherford was convinced that tenure lay at the heart of the educational malaise gripping the profession. While at Stanford, he had supervised a graduate-student research project that determined 65 percent of tenured faculty members (across all disciplines) decreased their scholarly output (research, publications, grants) by up to 50 percent within five years of earning tenure. The report also found that tenured faculty's student ratings dropped by an average 20 percent within two years of receiving tenure.

Blaine had convinced the SU regents that their problems at SU could have been avoided if the president had the power to dismiss inept, incompetent, and nonproductive faculty members. He also yanked the authority to grant faculty promotions from the sacrosanct faculty committees and invested that authority in independent, nationally recognized experts who served on national committees. He had always considered the tradition of faculty deciding each other's promotion and tenure as akin to intellectual incest.

Lane felt a surge of energy and anticipation as he contemplated getting back to work.

Meanwhile, Steve finished stacking the newly delivered firewood on the front porch. He still had not adjusted to losing the sun so early in the day. It was already beginning to slip behind Baker Mountain, and it was only four in the afternoon. The shadows grew long, and the brisk afternoon air would soon turn frigid. The nighttime temperature would drop into the low thirties even this late in the year.

He carried a fresh load of aspen firewood into the house. Steve had become the household expert at loading the old-fashioned wood stove just right and starting a fire that soon had the house baking. He placed one log of pinon in with the aspen. The aspen caught fire quickly and burned hot and fast, while the pinon took longer to ignite but would burn slowly. The right combination of firewood would burn all night and still be glowing in the early morning hours.

Steve enjoyed the isolation of their new home, but he was lonely. The kids were friendly enough, but Steve was introverted, and he found it difficult to make new friends. His quiet manner was often misinterpreted as aloofness or conceit, and coming from a foreign country (Texas) made it even more difficult to be accepted. The ski resort had become his own debutant ball though. He had always been extremely coachable, and he took to the slopes with abandon. On slow days (of which there were many), Greg Wilson, head of the ski patrol, instructed him.

The LaVeta school held classes Monday through Thursday. Almost all students depended on the bus for transportation. By going a few minutes longer for four days and taking Friday off, the district conserved a lot of bus fuel and utilities. Steve used the extra day wisely. He had no trouble with his studies, so he was able to spend the extra time on skis. By the end of the ski season, Steve was practicing with the local ski team, negotiating the slalom course with confidence, and making practice runs with the ski patrol's long red sled, which was used to transport injured skiers down the slopes to the first-aid clinic at the base of the mountain. Greg even invited him to ski with the Junior ski patrol next winter. The mountain had turned out to be a wonderful matchmaker, and Steve had become a member of Cuchara's first ski "gang."

The gang's leadership shifted effortlessly among the three skiers, depending on who had the most brazen idea for that day. When the slopes were choked with tourists, this fearsome threesome delighted in skiing with seemingly choreographed blazing speed below the longest ski lift. The tourists, many of whom were taking their first ski lessons, watched them in awe from the lifts. Greg had firmly cautioned them on more than one occasion to slow down. After skiing with them on several occasions though, he came to realize they were always in control and soon stopped worrying about them or the other skiers. Cold-weather skiing called for plenty of protection (stocking caps, sun glasses, or goggles and jackets) that was, if not fashionable, at least colorful. The ski gang soon had adopted its own "colors," which could be seen for miles. Hence, they were always recognized and greeted by strangers when they took a break in the warming hut. Strangers' reactions were dominated by surprise at their youth and skiing ability and by delight once they engaged the three in conversation. They became the ski resort's best PR tool, dispensing advice about the snow conditions on all the ski runs, the best ski instructors, weather forecasts, or the best brand and length of ski to use. Tourists were always eager to talk to locals: about where they went to school, what it was like to live near a ski resort, what the summers were like, as if they were visiting Never-Never-Land and had just met Peter Pan.

Now that the ski season was coming to an end, Steve wasn't sure what to expect. Both Tom Evers and John Dixon, his partners in skiing, had to work during the summers. Tom helped his dad with the family construction business. John, who lived with his mother, was going to work for the groundskeeper of the new golf course in LaVeta. That's just what kids in LaVeta and the outlying areas did—they worked when they weren't in school. None of them (legally) drove yet, so Steve was sad as he thought about a summer without them.

Spring awakens slowly and majestically in Colorado's high country, chasing winter away with warm days that swell the creeks and rivers with fast-moving snow melt. Winter is always reluctant to go, however, and often turns on spring like a playful cur suddenly snapping with rage at being hurried out. Old-timers like to tell about the year that the Fourth of July softball game at Cuchara Pass was snowed out. It is not unusual for an Albuquerque Low to squat over New Mexico in late March or even early April and drop thirty inches of fat, wet snow on Cuchara. June 1 is the earliest recommended date to put plants outdoors. Eventually, spring prevails and the green of the aspens rushes up the mountain sides like wildfire.

THE RANCHO NOT SO GRANDE

Lane turned off LaVeta's main street and headed west on a dirt road that spewed thick dust as he accelerated. He wanted to do something special for Steve's first official summer day. Lane worried constantly about his son and how he was coping. Steve was very private and never complained, so Lane didn't know if he was adjusting to their new home, to the school, to mountain living. This was so unlike what either of them was used to. The cold could be brutal at times, the temperature routinely plunging below zero, even bottoming out near minus thirty degrees during one near blizzard in February. But their southern location also enjoyed some surprisingly mild days when temperatures would soar into the fifties. It was those days that gave the ski resort management fits as they watched their "white gold" melt and run into Baker Creek. He and Steve had soon learned how to dress for winter: layers of warm clothing, stocking caps, gators, and good gloves. Nonetheless, they were eager for spring and that day they celebrated its arrival.

Chris had told him about Reggie Austin, one of the valley's experienced wranglers. She was taking her horses out for the season's first trail ride into the mountains to condition the horses, which had been lollygagging all winter and getting fat on alfalfa hay. She also wanted to orient the rookies on how to behave around the veteran horses and to get them used to riders again.

"Dad, is this ranch some kind of joke? The Rancho Not So Grande? What is that about?" Steve asked with a doubtful smile.

"From what Chris tells me, Reggie looks at the world through different eyes than most everyone else. She is a true cowgirl and a master horseman—not too hung up on politically correct gender issues either—and in fact is as disdainful of PC as anyone can get. She is very good at what she does and has complete confidence in where she is in life. And everyone else knows it too. She lives a very simple life, and the name of her ranch is probably meant as a poke in the eye of the larger family ranches around here. She doesn't take herself too seriously," Lane said half in response to Steve and half in conversation with himself. "Her real name is Regina, but she's let it be known that she'll hurt anyone who ever calls her that. Her friends know she's bluffing, sort of, but no one has ever called her bluff.

"She owns ten to fifteen horses and uses them in the summer tourist trail rides. During hunting season, she guides hunting parties on horseback, sets up their hunting camps, and helps them pack their deer or elk out of the wilderness. She also instructs for the ski resort during the winter to earn extra money for keeping her horses in feed. Chris says she works harder than most men he knows."

They drove in silence for ten or fifteen minutes, trying to take in the early, frosty Colorado morning. Lane was in constant awe of the sky here, words like "clear" just did not do it justice. He had never seen this shade of blue—anywhere. It was like God had invented it just for Cuchara. He searched his sizeable vocabulary: "brilliant," "intense," "wow" seemed the most fitting tributes.

Lane slowed and rechecked the crude map Chris had drawn for him.

"Here it is." He turned onto a narrow dirt road. At the end of the driveway (really more of a two lane trail) stood a small wooden frame house surrounded by aspen trees, their new spring leaves shimmering and dancing in the breeze. Lane pulled over so the Suburban would not block the way. He and Steve got out and stood for a minute, looking around. A small, sturdy barn stood about fifty feet from the house. Several horses were tethered to the fence, munching hay. They glanced disinterestedly at the new arrivals. The main entrance to the barn opened into a pen that looked like it could hold fifteen or twenty horses without crowding them. Behind the barn stretched an open meadow for a good five acres or so covered in tall grass that sparkled with the morning dew. More horses grazed there, all intent on the task at hand.

A slender—no—wiry woman strode out of the barn, carrying a saddle and blanket. She walked up to a beautiful mare. The mare turned her head, and the woman held the saddle-and-blanket combination up as if for inspection while the mare performed a cursory visual and smell test. Apparently, it passed inspection. Reggie eased the blanket onto the mare's back, tugged it forward slightly, and patted it down. She then swung the saddle up and adjusted it to the blanket. With practiced and effortless movements, she cinched the saddle down tightly and carefully fit the bridle into the mare's mouth.

Steve and Lane began walking toward the barn somewhat in awe of someone with such mastery of the western art of horsemanship. As they drew near, Lane could see Reggie more clearly. Hair in two tight pigtails, blue jeans, scuffed and crusty cowboy boots), a red and gray plaid shirt, and a hunting knife snugged prominently in a leather scabbard on her belt. Topping off the ensemble was a well-worn, slightly battered cowboy hat.

"You must be Reggie," Lane said. "I'm Lane Curry and this is Steve. Anything we can do to help?"

"You're the city slickers, right?" Reggie smiled and walked toward them, extending her calloused hand. She focused on Steve first.

"Do you like horses, Steve?" She shook Steve's hand.

"I love horses. I haven't been on one since I was five or six though," Steve answered.

"Well, you're gonna be fine. I'm putting you on Silver. See the third mare right over there, the one with the silver-looking mane? She's my most experienced trail horse, very responsive to her rider. She's a real sweetheart; not only that, she's a new mom."

Steve craned his neck to see around the other horses. Now he could see a small foal nursing.

"Whoa. Would she let me get closer?"

"Well, you gotta get closer to ride her. Come on. You too, Lane."

Lane was probably as excited as Steve. He was a horse lover too and loved riding. This was as good as it got.

Reggie walked up to Silver first, stroked her nose, and spoke softly to her.

"Hey, sweet mama. How's baby doing today?" The foal continued nursing. Silver nuzzled Reggie as Lane and Steve approached. Steve ran his hand along her flank and moved to her front.

"Hi, Silver. How nice to meet you."

Reggie untied the bridle and handed it to Steve.

"Here. You lead her out front by the trailer. We have to drive a ways first."

Steve led Silver out of the pen as the frisky foal trotted along behind, neighing and snorting.

Lane observed, "He's probably the happiest kid on earth right now. He also may be one of the most inexperienced riders on earth. I hope we don't slow you down."

"I take all kinds of riders out. Steve strikes me as a sensible one. These horses are very gentle and trail-wise. This early in the season, the younger, less experienced horses will be pretty frisky, but not Silver. I'm putting you on Thunder. This gelding right here. Why don't you saddle him up?"

Under Reggie's watchful eye and with practiced coaching, Lane had Thunder saddled up and cinched without causing too much distress to himself or to the horse. There was one other family of riders and a young man who would be assisting Reggie with her trail rides during the summer, six riders in all. Reggie trailered the horses and told the riders to follow her as her beaten-up Toyota mini truck didn't have room for all of them. Lane offered to carry the other riders with him and Steve.

"My name's Ellen Bell and this is my son Tommy. We're visiting the Raineys in Pine Haven," Ellen Bell held out her hand. Her young son looked about seven or eight years old. He shook hands all around. They drove for about twenty minutes behind Reggie's trailer before she stopped, got out, and opened a gate. Steve jumped out to close it behind the caravan.

Steve cradled his boot in the stirrup and pulled himself into the saddle. Silver seemed not to notice. Reggie addressed the group of riders.

"Everybody pay attention, please. You get to hear my world-famous riding speech, whether you need it or not. Horses are not terribly smart. They mostly operate on instinct and intuition, but they do learn, and they sense their riders very keenly. Mostly, they want the rider to tell them what to do. Use the heels of your boots against their sides, like this, and they will move forward." She tapped Jeddi's sides and he moved ahead briskly.

"To stop, put gentle, even back pressure on the reins. Remember, the bit is putting pressure on the soft tissue in the back of their mouths, so you don't need to use force especially with these horses."

Reggie began a right turn. "See how I'm laying the left rein against the left side of Jeddi's neck? I'm also gently pressuring his left side with my left knee. He knows I want him to turn to the right." Reggie did a 360-degree turn and then a turn to the left. She then backed Jeddi straight back for a few feet.

"Horses can also be stubborn. Just like people. They can also be lazy. The rider has to let their horse know they're in charge at all times. If you don't, they can make your lives miserable. Is everybody ready?" Reggie wheeled Jeddi, a magnificent coal black gelding, around and headed the caravan. Lane went next with Steve behind him, with Tommy and his mom trailing him, and Todd, Reggie's helper-in-training, taking up the rear.

Steve was exhilarated. His initial anxiety melted away as he felt Silver respond to his subtle instructions. Reggie had brought along Silver's foal, Sweet Pea, to expose her to trail rides and so that Silver would be more at ease. Sweet Pea nestled up close to Silver's right flank when they started moving. It was close to 9:00 a.m., and even though it had been daylight since about 7:00, the sun was still behind the mountains and the air still carried a frosty bite. They had walked at a brisk pace on the two-lane dirt path for about thirty minutes when Reggie led them into a meadow of high grass and wildflowers. A few minutes of easy riding brought them to a small but full and noisy creek. The spring melt had filled it to capacity. The water couldn't have been much more than a foot deep and the grassy banks were only two to three feet apart. The riders watched Jeddi propel himself slightly off the ground and clear the creek with a powerful jump. Reggie turned him around so she was facing them and encouraged Lane, "Give him his head, tap his sides, and let him do the rest. Use your legs to hold on to the saddle so you won't jostle too much when he lands." Lane's horse, Thunder, cleared the creek effortlessly. Steve followed with Ellen right behind. Reggie had moved them away from the creek to avoid a traffic jam, and they were all watching and waiting for young Tommy to follow. But his mare, Daisy, just stood there grazing. Todd was encouraging Tommy and giving him instructions to no avail. Reggie watched for a couple of minutes. "Well, let's move on. He knows what to do, and maybe when he sees us leaving, he'll get his act in gear."

Ellen said, "I'll go back and talk to him." She was uncertain about what to do but couldn't bring herself to leave her young son in the wilderness on a horse that wouldn't obey.

"No. That'll just make it worse," Reggie semi-barked at her. "We won't go far. He'll be fine." Reggie had a domineering presence, and she spoke in commands when she wanted her riders or her horses to do something. That was that. They rode about thirty yards away. Reggie stopped, and they turned around. Tommy was still there. Todd was riding to catch up in a leisurely trot. "He just won't budge. He says he's afraid of falling in the water. I think Daisy is just being lazy or else she's spooked by the noisy creek," Todd reported to Reggie with a bemused look.

Reggie believed that people of all ages, like horses, needed to do the right thing at the right time. She was always cocked for action rather than words. Steve was beside her and noticed when she leaned forward slightly. Jeddi exploded into a full gallop, his hooves spraying dirt and grass in the air behind him. They covered the distance to the creek with a thunder of hooves, and Jeddi flew over the little creek with amazing grace. Reggie pulled Jeddi right next to Daisy, who stutter-stepped slightly in surprise. They could see Reggie's face, by now in an animated scowl, but could only hear bits and pieces of the one-sided conversation, "Holding . . . up . . . everybody . . . ass . . . moving . . . g . . . d . . . horse . . . that creek . . . now!

Lane leaned over toward Steve and said, "Now I know how nuclear fission works." Both he and Steve suppressed smiles in deference to Ellen who just sat and watched stoically. Daisy jumped the creek with ease once Tommy put his heels into her sides. They trotted up to the crowd. Reggie did not say a word and went to the front of the group. The rest of the day, Tommy and Daisy got along famously. Ellen later confided to Lane, "That's exactly what his father would have done."

They were soon in a gentle climb in and out of the aspen trees. There was no trail that Steve could see. They strolled through meadows into heavy trees. One aspen forest was so tight that the riders had to squeeze their legs tightly to the saddles to fit between the giant trees. Reggie would stop now and then to allow the horses to catch their breath as they were in a constant climb. Steve had always thought horses could just run forever, but he began to realize they were like any other athletes and had to train and condition. About noon, they broke out of the trees into a high mountain meadow with a breathtaking view of the Sangre de Cristo mountain range dominated by Raspberry Mountain.

"Welcome to the dining room," Reggie called out. "Let's have lunch."

Todd retrieved the boxed lunches, and they spread out on the ground to eat. The horses began some serious grazing after drinking deeply from a small stream. Steve had never seen such awesome landscape. The snow-covered peaks piercing the brilliant blue sky were breathtaking. The floor of the meadow was just breaking out in a variety of wild flowers—red, yellow, blue, and purple. Sweet Pea had overcome her initial shyness and was wandering further and further from Silver. She would run two or three steps and kick her hind legs, then run another few steps and launch straight-legged into the air. Silver kept a watchful and patient eye on her and would occasionally whinny softly. Steve noticed the exuberant young foal, as adventuresome as she was now, still made short trips back to mama. They would exchange nuzzles and Sweet Pea, emboldened again, would strike out on her own sun-speckled adventure.

Lane asked Reggie what their schedule was for the day. She replied that it was to start the trail ride after sunrise and end it before sunset. Beyond that, there was no itinerary. Lane smiled and willingly accepted the mild rebuke. This was not a menu-driven city bus tour.

Reggie saddled them up and led them north along a piney mountain ridge for several miles. Hooves crunched the remnants of the season's last snow as they began the day's first descent. Soon they were ankle deep in snow, protected from the sun's warmth by giant ponderosa pine trees. Single-file, they tramped down the narrow trail. A steep, rocky embankment jutted up on their right. Dense aspen trees crowded them on the left as the terrain dropped off sharply. Steve could swing his arms out and almost touch the opposite sides of their mountain corridor. Reggie took the rear so she could see everyone. She was surprised at the amount of snow left and wished, too late, that she had taken them on the longer but more moderate trail down. Fortunately, she had put Tommy on Ellen's horse, anticipating the steepness of their descent, but was concerned about Steve's ability to keep his cool on the narrow and slippery trail. She could not ride next to him due to the terrain. Reggie would have to rely on his being able to follow her instructions and hope he would keep his cool. The horses were slipping and sliding on the snowy rocks.

Lane did not want to think about the catastrophe of a horse sliding out of control and scattering riders off the trail and through the trees. He could hear Reggie instructing Steve on technique. Her voice was as calm as it was when she told him how to cinch the saddle.

"Steve, give Silver her head. Let the reins hang loose. Lean slightly back in the saddle and take your feet out of the stirrups. If she stumbles and starts to fall, be sure and jump to the right side, the uphill side."

Steve was anxious but not frightened. He could feel the frigid mountain air cooling the sweat on his forehead. There was nothing in his world but the trail and the horse and her every movement. He trusted Silver and felt her power and strength under him as she fought to keep her balance. She seemed to know when to accept the sliding and when to deny it with subtle shifts of weight. Steve felt as one with her, and it was the most exhilarating experience of his life.

Soon the trees gave way to an open meadow and the trail became wider and flatter. The horses fanned out and, sensing they were on the way home, began fidgeting and quickened their pace. Reggie let Jeddi run. Thunder and Silver both lengthened their strides to keep up with Jeddi. Hooves thundered on the dirt trail as the day's shadows stretched ahead of them. Lane could hear Thunder's heaving breath. He was in awe of the power under him and around him as the three horses surged forward. After a short sprint, Reggie reined in Jeddi, and all the horses settled into a comfortable gait. Lane looked over to Steve who was riding just slightly ahead. He could swear that Steve was riding just a little taller and straighter in the saddle than when they started out that morning.

After they helped Reggie unsaddle the horses and put out their feed, Reggie came over and hugged Steve.

"Hey, cowboy, you can ride on my trail ride anytime."

Lane turned away quickly and walked briskly to the Suburban.

GROWING

Summer creeps up on the Cuchara Valley. It meanders up the mountain sides, splashing color everywhere as the aspen leaves break out in their bright greens. It traipses through the meadows and sprinkles dazzling hues of mountain flowers to accent the deepening green of grass.

Steve had grown three inches and put on ten pounds since moving to LaVeta. He had skied hard while the resort was open and played baseball for the LaVeta Redskins. Lane had noticed that Steve walked and even spoke with a newfound confidence. He seemed to be fitting in their new environment and making friends. His grades were good, and he willingly took on new chores, especially those involving lifting, carrying, or splitting fire wood, which seemed to be never ending. Even as the days of June grew warmer, the nights often dipped well below freezing.

Steve still had his own emotional hiding place. The place he had found soon after his mom died. He allowed no one to enter. Lane had screwed up his own courage and tried several times to no avail. Like summer clouds rushing to cover the sun, Steve's face would cloud over, protecting that place.

Steve could not have explained it. He had never been very expressive or demonstrative, and his mother had been the only one who could open him up. She saw right into him, sensed his moods, and entered his heart with her soft yet probing questions. He would pour it all out to her, and she always understood exactly what he was trying to say even when he stammered, mumbled, or stumbled his way through it. Now that she was gone, his words and his soul just could not find their way. The path was too dark.

Lane had also developed a routine, sort of. He had improvised an office out of an empty retail space at the resort. The resort owners were glad to have someone on the premises and provided the space and the minimal utilities at no charge. Lane had thrown himself into developing his fall course for the university. His colleagues had started pestering him with book ideas, and he had renewed his daily reading habit. Like his son, though, he lived his days in a shadow of grief with only occasional glimpses of the sun.

"Dad! Are you there?" Steve called out as he burst into the house. He half jogged to the back door and threw it open.

"Dad! Guess what!" He saw Lane at the back of the lot stacking firewood. Lane turned toward him with an armful of split aspen logs and headed his way.

"I got a job. I'm going to work for Don Emmons at the Wild Horse Corral. You know that old empty building at the resort entrance? Well, Don, uh Mr. Emmons, is gonna set up his wrangler headquarters, you know, so he can take tourists on trail rides and cookouts. He said he needs someone who's not afraid of horses to help him feed them, bridle them, and walk them from the corral to be saddled, and even help saddle them, the short ones that is. He'll pay me some but will let me ride for free mostly." Steve paused only because he ran out of breath.

"What do you think? He said I needed to clear it with you. Oh, yeah—I also have to shovel horse sh—, uh manure."

Lane just stood there taking it all in. His son's exuberance was intoxicating. Steve had never been this excited. He replied to Steve, "It sounds like a dream job. Can you get me hired too?"

THE WILD HORSE CORRAL

Steve's summer days began at 6:30 a.m. when he arrived at the Wild Horse Corral to feed the horses. The horses were anything but wild. Don had trained them to be very gentle and forgiving. It wasn't really much of a corral either. Don had built it himself out of aspen and cedar logs, very sturdy and very Western looking. Part of Steve's job was to keep it clean and neat looking, which involved a lot of shoveling. He also kept the saddles neatly lined up on the covered front porch of the office building along with all the bridles and reins. The horses needed fresh water daily. Steve hauled it up from Baker Creek, which gurgled swiftly just a few yards from the corral. He also learned to guesstimate when they would run out of feed and hay and alert Don. Before long, Don had taught him how to brush the horses, how to slip the bridles into the backs of their mouths without hurting them (or getting bitten), how to position the blankets, and how to saddle and cinch properly. At first, Steve had to stand on a big cedar stump to be able to swing a saddle over the shortest horse, but by summer's end, he could easily swing one up and onto the back of the tallest horse, Diamond.

Steve also learned that horses are not always fun to be around. Once, Caesar, a big black gelding, ate too many green apples and got very ill. Don had to take out a big trail ride with ten riders, and he left Steve with stern instructions, "Do not let Caesar lay down whatever you have to do. Keep him up on his feet and walking until we get back."

The first hour was not too bad. Steve walked Caesar all up and down the trails, crisscrossing Baker Creek, up and down the road from Highway 12 to the resort until the traffic made that too dangerous for both of them. Suddenly, Caesar's knees buckled, and he went down on his right side with a heavy thud. Steve jumped out of the way and ran to Caesar's head. He pulled his head up and toward him. Caesar didn't budge. Steve faced the big horse, pulling the reins toward himself. Nothing. Caesar's breathing grew heavy and labored. He seemed to be in real distress. Steve was close to panic and fought back tears of frustration. He squeezed his arms beneath Caesar's neck and pushed upward as hard as he could. He could feel the big horse struggle, his hot breath raspy and wheezing. Steve was on his knees trying to move his feet in closer under his body for more pushing power. He gave a mighty shove to the massive neck, and Caesar craned his neck forward. Steve felt progress and moved his entire body with the momentum. Caesar was trying to get his feet under him. Steve shifted quickly to the front and grabbed the horse's head, pulling it toward him. With a giant lurch, Caesar was up on all four feet, shaking the dirt off and whinnying loudly. Steve almost kissed him on his big slobbery mouth. He picked up the reins and slowly walked Caesar back to the corral. He could see Don leading the returning riders across Baker Creek. Steve worked furiously to regain his composure.

Don often took Steve along on the smaller trail rides and taught him the art of horsemanship. Steve never tired of being on horseback even though his legs and butt ached the next day. They rode to places most visitors to the valley could only dream about. Steve also enjoyed meeting the tourists. Most of them were true city slickers and loved to meet someone who lived in Cuchara, especially a youngster like Steve, an accomplished horseman who possessed formidable knowledge of the area (gleaned from hours of listening to Don). Steve's confidence grew daily. Don even let him take out experienced riders by himself for short rides.

Don Emmons was a renaissance cowboy, if there ever was one. Like many immigrants to Cuchara, Don had relocated his family looking for a new start. A successful rancher in Hereford, Texas, Don had gotten overwhelmed financially just as the cattle economy was crashing. He lost his ranch and all of his equipment to foreclosure. Fortunately, his dad and partner had kept all the horses and a few head of cattle in his own name, so over several months, Don relocated all he owned to Cuchara. He started a very small cattle operation on leased acreage and a trail riding business on Cuchara and National Forest land in the summer. During the winter, he would rent snow mobiles and guide tourists over many of the snow-covered horse riding trails. He was such a natural and gifted mechanic that the resort hired him to supervise the ski lift maintenance crews.

It didn't take long for Lane to discover Don was also a rather imposing intellectual. He seemed interested in absolutely everything and had read something about most of it. His son Michael was an engineering student at the elite Colorado School of Mines in Golden, Colorado.

Lane began showing up at the Wild Horse Corral to check up on Steve and to help Don out with menial chores. He loved being around the horses and listening to Don talk about their personalities and how he had to treat them all differently much like a group of teenagers.

"But," he remarked once, "the horses are much better behaved than some of the tourists."

Steve invited Lane to come along on one of Don's famous dinner rides in early June. The summer residents were filling up their family cabins, some for the entire summer. Don offered a family-oriented dinner ride, which included riding in a Western-style wagon to the outdoor cook site, cowboy cooking, and live entertainment. Don baked delicious pies in a Dutch oven and fired up a giant barbecue grill filled with mesquite logs for the hamburgers and chicken. Willie Baxter, a true Cuchara local, would strum a guitar and sing cowboy songs or recite cowboy poetry. Willie looked and dressed the part of a frontier mountain man. Those who knew him best joked that Willie improved his dress considerably for these outdoor affairs. He was a huge hit with the crowds. He had a natural, easy manner about him, and he added a romantic reminder of the original settlers of Cuchara Valley.

Even the ride to the "dining room" captivated the guests. Don used two Belgian draft horses named Charley and Chubby to pull the wagon. One of the gentlest breeds, Belgians often reached a height of eighteen hands and could weigh up to two thousand pounds. Lane was surprised to learn the pair would only pull when Charley was on the left side. Charley and Chubby usually pulled the wagon with fifteen to twenty guests up the grassy trail that wound its way in a steady climb through a thick aspen grove. Don had installed his outdoor kitchen in a small meadow at the edge of the aspens where the terrain leveled out, guiding the eye straight to Trinchera Peak, soaring over 13,500 feet to the south. By the time Charley and Chubby delivered the evening's dinner guests, Don's son, Michael, had the cook fire roaring and the Dutch ovens baking. Willie would usually warm up the guests with a mournful ballad about a long-ago forbidden love affair between a beautiful Ute Indian princess and a young Spanish priest. Willie would end the song in Spanish, the lyrics wringing tears from even the most cynical eye.

Drinks were iced down in a decrepit horse trough. A collection of chain-sawed stumps, clustered in groups of four or five, served as dining tables and were just high enough for diners to sit cross-legged on the high meadow grass. The dining fare was always the same: charcoal braised chicken, hamburgers, and baked beans bubbling in one of the Dutch ovens. Cherry and peach cobblers, too hot to eat, soon cooled in the crisp mountain air.

Steve mostly helped Michael prep the site and the fires. He would also browse among the guests, offering to get them drinks, answering the usual tourist questions:

"Do you think we'll see any bears tonight?"

"Oh, the bears are all over. I wouldn't be surprised. Just be sure not to wander too far from the group," Steve would say with a half grin. He had learned how to enthrall the tourists.

Lane had joined the dinner ride on a spectacular night. Just as darkness crept over the valley, the full moon rose and lit up Trinchera Peak like a spotlight, its snowy peak glistening. The moon was red and huge and seemed to glide across the starry night sky. Lane, along with the other guests, was transfixed. After a few breathless "wows," the entire group stood in silent awe, mindful of their smallness.

THE GATHERING

Whoop, whoop, whoop, whoop. Steve was preoccupied with building his very first log cabin, so the distant noise did not register. Sampson, the big Chesapeake Bay retriever, roused from his daytime snooze and was on instant alert. Ever since Lane had surprised Steve with a brown furry puppy, Sampson had been his constant companion. He growled softly, trying to associate the strange sounds with some imminent danger. The sounds grew louder and closer, and Sampson grew nervous and began pacing and whining. "Sampson, what is it?" Steve could now hear the heavy beating of the air and the roar of an engine as something very large moved up the valley toward him. He strained his neck back and tried to see between the aspen leaves. All at once, a gigantic green monster swooped overhead with a deafening roar. Steve took off running with Sampson, who was now barking furiously, close behind. Sampson soon passed him and charged ahead into a large meadow ringed by aspen trees, blue fir, and ponderosa pines. Sampson was engulfed in a gale force wind but stood his ground, ready to defend Steve to the death. The cacophony of noise drowned out his frantic barking as Steve rushed to his side. "Whoa! It's a Chinook, Sampson!" He grabbed Sampson's collar and watched as the giant army helicopter settled onto the ground, its huge twin rotors winding down. A whirlwind of dirt, leaves, and semi-melted snow surrounded the beast. Several men, the Colorado sun glinting off their helmets, left the copter and began walking to the edge of the field where Steve could see a group of grown-ups waiting.

The crowd was mostly locals whom Steve recognized at once. He had to see the helicopter crew up close, so he approached with a purposeful stride that he reckoned to be less childlike than running. As he approached the crowd, he could see they were preparing for some kind of search and rescue. Cuchara's ancient four-wheel drive rescue truck was parked on the road, and there was Chris with his cross-country skis and his personal rescue pack. After introductions, the men spread a topographical map across the weather-scarred hood of the rescue truck. "This is where the Blue Lake Road intersects the trail to Trinchera Peak. If he drove up there, as we believe he did, he had to go this way. There's a cut-off to the Purgatoire Trail about a mile and a half beyond this point. There's a lot of territory to cover. We need your help. If you can find any signs at all of the direction he may have taken, it might make the difference between rescuing a lost camper and recovering his body." Chris was addressing the flight crew. They were stationed at Fort Carson, the army post in Colorado Springs, and provided assistance to search and rescue crews all over the state of Colorado. They could cover much more ground from the air and direct the rescue team in the right direction. If they located the camper and could find a suitable landing zone nearby, they could pick him up themselves, otherwise they would direct the ground rescue crew to the location.

Steve inched closer. He was in awe of these air warriors and their flying skills. The Army CH-47 Chinook looked menacing even in a state of silent repose, with its giant twin rotors drooping. The crew would have been impressed with Steve's technical knowledge of their craft. Since Steve could remember, he had been fascinated with aircraft and read anything and everything about them. The Boeing CH-47 (MH-47 for special forces) was fifty-one feet long, eighteen feet and eleven inches tall, and sported twin rotors with a sixty-foot span. Each one of the twin T55 turbine engines produced three thousand horsepower. These babies could cruise at 143 knots at their maximum gross weight of 50,000 pounds and climb at a rate of over 1,500 feet per minute. The Chinook could carry up to fifty-five troops (after special seating was installed) and could transport everything from howitzers to Humvees in a sling load (a series of straps attached to the bottom of the fuselage). It was the fastest helicopter in the army's fleet, and it was sitting in Steve's meadow, beckoning him to take the pilot's seat and fly into the wild blue Colorado yonder.

Sampson was less impressed. Now that he was no longer in his protect-to-the-death mode, his tail wagged lazily as he sniffed each strange pair of boots. Occasionally, one of the strangers would give him a friendly rub and a kind word, "Good dog." He found a familiar scent and looked up expectantly. Chris was occupied and ignored him. Sampson moved on. There was tension in the voices that made him a little uneasy. He found a sunny spot and curled up with his big head resting on his paws where he could keep Steve in his sight.

Chesapeake Bay retrievers develop extraordinary loyalty to their human counterparts. They are a sociable, working breed descended from a mixture of Newfoundlands and other working dogs. People often mistake them for a Lab or traditional retriever because of their large heads and intelligent, knowing eyes. Actually, there is no familial connection to Labs or retrievers. Their short, sometimes curly fur often attracts attention. Underneath that soft exterior is a coating of oil that helps insulate their skin from wet and cold. So an exuberant plunge into icy water was no big deal for Sampson. They tolerate strangers well, but transform into protectors quickly and aggressively if their territory or "family" is threatened. Sampson weighed in at close to 115 pounds of muscle and blind courage. He and Steve were inseparable. The pair brought to mind the maxim "Every boy needs a dog," or was it "Every dog needs a boy"? Either way, it's one of life's truths.

The crowd around the truck began to dissipate, and Steve moved toward Chris. "Hey, Chris," he called as nonchalantly as he could. "Hey, buddy," Chris waved at him. "How do you like the present I ordered for ya?" gesturing to the Chinook. "You gotta promise to take me for a ride someday." Chris was grinning. He knew how thrilled Steve must be at his proximity to such a wonderful piece of flying machinery and its crew. He could never resist the temptation to good-naturedly tease Steve because he was normally such a reserved and serious boy. Chris also recognized the undeniable hero worship that Steve carried for him. Beneath his teasing, sometimes flippant demeanor, Chris took that responsibility very seriously.

"You know I can't take you up until you're a qualified Chinook freak," Steve shot back. Changing his tone, he asked, "What's going on?"

"A camper has been missing for about seven days. He was supposed to call his roommate back in Nashville three days ago. The roommate waited a day then notified the camper's parents." Chris nodded his head toward a civilian that rode in with the Chinook crew. "That's his father. He's a retired air force general, and he pulled some strings at the Pentagon. That's why the Chinook's here. He remembers his son talking about Trinchera Peak before he left. That's all we know."

Steve became very quiet. Up until now, the missing camper had been a novelty, someone who had brought great fortune into the Cuchara Valley with his disappearance. The army's most awesome chopper and the excitement of a search and rescue were events of a lifetime. But knowing that the missing camper had a father and seeing the fatigue and worry on that father's face turned excitement into sober reality. Steve thought about how his dad would feel if he had been lost for seven days, and the prospect almost made him cry.

Chris continued, "The army is going to fly over Blue Lake and follow the trail to Trinchera, flying a grid pattern as long as their fuel holds out. We're gonna drive up to Blue Lake and meet Don, who'll have his horses ready to head out from there."

"How are they going to see anything through all the trees?" Steve asked.

"They know it's a long shot, and we know it's a long shot, but they got instructions to take a look. Maybe they'll see something. Who knows?" Chris shrugged.

Steve knew from reading about other searches in this part of the country and from overhearing Chris and others who made up the core search and rescue teams in Huerfano County that seven days was a lifetime in the rescue business. He knew without asking that Chris thought it was already too late. There was never a thought of not looking though. Blue Lake Campground was nestled among the pines at over 10,500 feet. The nightly temperatures would dip into the low teens even though it was early June.

Without thinking, Steve blurted out, "Chris, can I go with you? You know I'm a good rider, and I'll help Don with the horses. I need to start getting experience now if I'm ever going to be a search-and-rescue professional." Next to flying a Chinook, leading search-and-rescue expeditions was Steve's most earnest fantasy.

Chris made a mistake. He hesitated just a second before quashing the idea that Steve might actually go along. Steve sensed the ambivalence and launched the second attack. "What if Dad says it's okay?" Steve was firing blindly now. He knew that was not a good bet either, but he had a vague notion that the longer he could delay a downright refusal, the greater his chances of winning. Steve was big for his age and remarkably mature and responsible for a fourteen-year-old. Since he and his dad had moved to Cuchara, Colorado, three years ago, Steve had reveled in their mountain-resort life.

"I don't think so, buddy. This could turn out to be a gruesome task." Chris was trying to regain the advantage.

Steve was on the move. "I'll talk to Dad and we'll get back to you." He had to at least keep the momentum from turning against him. Sampson was up and moving, glad to be in action. They ran toward the now-empty ski slopes. Lane had his office in one of the resort's buildings.

They both crashed through the front door, running on adrenalin and boy-dog exuberance. Steve slowed down to a walk once inside the building. The place was empty as the ski season had ended and only a few employees were still working on the slopes, taking down fences and lift-tower pads. He didn't want to arrive at his dad's office out of breath and incoherent. Lane was thoughtful and deliberate and was often trying to calm his son down to get him to think before he blurted.

"Dad, what's up?" he asked as he walked into the office. *Easy now. I want to start this off with the right tone*, he thought. "Hi, Steve. Hey, Sampson. What are you two knuckleheads up to?" That was a good sign. He was in a good mood.

"Did you hear about the search and rescue? And the Chinook? Dad, it's almost in our back yard!" Steve semi-blurted.

"Well, I knew they were organizing a search party, but the Chinook was a surprise. I spoke to Chris right before he left to meet it. Have you gotten a ride yet?" Lane Curry teasingly asked his son.

"Dad, I was talking to Chris about possibly riding along with the search party. Sampson and I can be useful, and it'll be a really good experience for me, don't you think?" Lane immediately recognized his son's strategy. What a sharp kid. He was using Lane's own language to bolster his request. Steve knew Lane valued real-life experience (or as the academicians would say, experiential learning) and that he welcomed Steve's involvement in worthwhile activities. But this might be a bit of a stretch. Lane also knew they were likely to be recovering a body.

"Steve, I don't know about that. I'm not sure how it would look for the search party to take along a kid your age. Especially given the serious nature of this search. And I'm not sure you have any business being along on this particular one. You do realize there's a chance that camper is not alive?" Steve felt his chances dimming by the minute.

"Let me go talk to Chris about this before I decide for sure," Lane said. Hope was still alive!

They walked out front and saw the growing search party gathering in the parking lot. Steve heard the Chinook's big engines winding up, out of sight, but unmistakably preparing to take off.

"Man, oh man!" Steve shouted. The Chinook rose just above the tree tops, lumbering as it turned, and headed right for them, its rotors gaining speed and the noise level rising painfully. The monster in flight seemed to fill the entire sky. Sampson was barking frantically and running toward the approaching helicopter. Mercifully, it passed over and soon disappeared over Baker Mountain.

Chris Boone and Lane Curry made an odd couple to those who knew only one of them. To those who took the time and energy to understand both of them, it was obvious that the friendship grew from genuine mutual admiration and respect. Lane was fond of saying Chris was the oldest hippie in the world. A veteran of the anti-war protests of the sixties, he had been arrested several times. He had marched on Washington and survived the National Guard. With neither apologies nor regrets, he often discussed his beliefs and how he had followed his heart. He still believed that the government is basically corrupt, corporate America is wantonly raping the environment, individual freedom is our most cherished right (including the right to put any substance into one's own body that one deemed necessary for the pursuit of life, liberty, and happiness), and being indoors for any extended period was tantamount to dying. The thing about Chris, though, was that he could debate any of those volatile issues without getting emotional about them. Woe to the aspiring intellect that underestimated Chris, though, or tried to outwit him. Chris's IQ bordered on the obscene, and Lane had never encountered a more skilled debater. After several hours-long discussions, Lane realized he agreed with many of Chris's positions. Their disagreements lay in how they chose to deal with them. Chris had always attacked while Lane had intellectualized. Each man looked back on the other's past with some amusement.

Steve was drawn to Chris because Chris had never given up many of his kidlike qualities, yet he was an adult and moved in the adult world. They became fast friends, and Chris taught him how to ski downhill while towing the ski patrol sled used to transport injured skiers. Lane trusted Chris and was happy Steve had found someone he obviously admired. At the same time, Lane felt a measure of guilt about his own relationship with his son. He knew there was something missing between him and Steve, and Lane feared yielding any of his parental responsibility.

His wife's sudden and violent death four years ago cast a permanent shadow over their lives. Lane had done everything possible to help Steve through the horrible aftermath. He had used grief counselors, psychologists, and family counselors. Steve had worked through his grief, gotten angry, lashed out at everyone around him, become depressed, and had finally seemed to accept that he would have to live the rest of his life without his mother. But there was a no-man's land into which neither of them had ventured. At some point, they had stopped talking about Becky, and they had not discussed her death since moving here. It was almost as if they feared they would have to go through the grief again. Lane didn't know if he was too afraid of triggering those ragged emotions or if he was hiding from his own fears. He had been battling his own demons since her death and wasn't sure if he could handle Steve's too. The longer he ignored the issue, the easier it was to rationalize doing nothing.

The search-and-rescue team had set up a command post in Baker Creek Restaurant. Joe and Ernie, the proprietors, had opened the doors and were putting out some food supplies for Don to pack. No one could put together a pack trip as fast or as efficiently as Don, the owner/operator of the Wild Horse Corral. He would lead the search because they would use his horses, and he knew the area inside and out. Chris would direct the search activities and any medical procedures, but Don would be in charge of the horses and the meals. Everyone on the team knew exactly what to do and who was in charge of what. Don didn't hesitate when he saw Lane and Steve heading for the restaurant.

"Lane," he drawled, "can you and Steve come along? I have two new horses that I really need to get trail-broke and Michael is still at school." Michael served as Don's right-hand man on all of the overnight trail rides. "I really need Steve to help me with the horses and all my gear. I also need a dependable rider to lead the pack animals," meaning Lane.

Steve was speechless. He couldn't believe that he was being recruited to go along! His dad would not be able to resist going himself because he prided himself on being a capable horseman and always being available to help out friends. Steve didn't dare open his mouth.

"Are you sure Steve won't be in the way?" Lane responded.

He was in, Steve thought. That was a weak question. Not even a protest. He tried to avoid looking at Don.

"Nope, I need him to help. We'll meet at Blue Lake at two o'clock sharp."

Lane and Steve shared a growing sense of adventure as they drove home to get dressed and pack for at least a two-day pack trip. There would be nine riders. Chris had been able to locate four other volunteers for the search-and-rescue crew, all trained as paramedics and in wilderness rescue techniques. The general was going along too. Chris had objected strenuously, but the general was used to getting his way, and his arguments were hard to counter. Chris didn't want to waste any more time arguing, so he acquiesced.

Warm clothing was the order of the day. Steve pulled on his long wool underwear and his thermal socks. He put on his waterproof, insulated boots. He wanted his dad to hurry so he could be the first one there to start helping Don right away. He was determined to prove to everyone that he was a serious participant in this venture and not just a tag-along kid.

THE SEARCH

The horses stamped their feet and snorted impatiently. Steve checked all the cinches one last time. He had to stretch his leg to reach the stirrup because Willie was a fairly tall horse. Willie pranced with excitement and shook his head when he felt Steve settle into the saddle. The horse wanted to get moving.

Don led them out. Lane followed, leading Jebediah, the only mule and the animal carrying the heaviest load. The packhorse fell in behind Jebediah, and the seasoned search members strung themselves into single file followed by their "guest," the general. Steve took up the rear because he was on Willie, not exactly a rookie on the trail, as Don had intimated. He and Willie had been partners before, usually riding in the rear. Don always wanted a stable, calm horse riding last in line with a rider who knew something about riding in the mountains. If one of the horses carrying a tourist got skittish and bolted up the trail into inexperienced riders, the other horses could panic, and Don would be too far ahead to do anything. Willie was a very calm and strong horse and would react quickly if Steve needed to move up next to a rider and help a younger or less-experienced trail horse. As much as Steve loved and enjoyed horses, they could be downright flaky at times.

They climbed steadily, with Don stopping often to let the horses catch their wind. They had been loafing all winter in Bruner's meadow and, with the occasional meal of alfalfa grass or sweet feed, had gotten fat. The trail was good and wide, and they meandered in and out of the shade of the giant pines. Weeks-old snow lingered in shady spots undisturbed until the onslaught of hooves. On and on, they climbed. Sampson wandered back and forth, crisscrossing left to right, right to left across the trail, always behind Willie. Don's Australian shepherd, Bear, stayed near the front, always within Don's sight and voice. The two dogs maintained their distance. They seemed to have an unspoken agreement to stay out of each other's space.

Bear was the most protective dog Steve had ever seen. He would tolerate you when he was with Don or Michael but stick your head in Don's truck when Bear was in charge, and he would try to tear your face off. Don loved telling the story of the rogue bull that charged his horse (while he was riding it) during spring roundup. Bear tore into the bull, grabbed its nose between his teeth, and would not let go. The poor bull didn't know what to do with this furry set of teeth clamped onto his nose. He froze and bellowed pitifully until Don called off Bear. Bear was half the size of Sampson but had a powerful ferocious streak and had laid waste to many a dog that had ventured too close. Steve smiled to himself as he remembered Sampson's introduction to Bear. He had taken Sampson for a walk through the ski-resort property about that same time of year when it was virtually deserted. Sampson was learning his obedience lessons and his manners but still reacted much like a puppy when someone approached. He wanted to run to them, greet them with a good slobbering, and be petted. They had stopped about twenty feet from where Don and a group of guest riders were going to pass. Steve grabbed Sampson's collar so he wouldn't have a chance to run toward the horses and spook them. This was a good training opportunity for Sampson. He had to learn to behave around horses. "Easy, Sampson. Stay." Steve used his master's voice and held Sampson tight. Bear had spotted them. Bear crouched low and came quickly toward them. Don had not seen what was about to happen. Bear zeroed in on this strange dog in his territory (which was defined by wherever Bear was or wanted to be). Sampson continued wagging his tail, ready to play with a new friend. Steve didn't know what to do. He didn't think he should release Sampson; it was up to him to control his dog, but he didn't like Bear's expression. Bear quickened his gait straight toward Sampson. Steve had to make a decision. He wasn't about to hold Sampson up for a frontal attack, and he knew how dangerous it could be in the middle of a dogfight. He released Sampson, who by now realized he was the object of attack. Sampson braced himself and bared his teeth. Bear went straight for his throat. The dogs met in a storm of snarling, snapping teeth and flying fur. It lasted less than a heartbeat. Bear yelped sharply and was then silent as Sampson stood over him like a conquering gladiator. "Sampson, come, boy," Steve commanded. Sampson released Bear who scurried off to rejoin the trail ride. Don didn't say anything, and Steve never mentioned it again. But he knew that Bear's world had just changed. The two dogs never played together, but Bear never challenged him again either. They tolerated each other while on trail rides, keeping a respectful distance from one another.

Other than the task facing the riders, the day was perfect. The cobalt blue sky was dazzling. The thin air was crisp and cool on their faces even as the sun sneaked through and around the towering pines. There was a rhythm to their procession as the horses clip-clopped along the trail, scattering the dregs of leftover snow. The riders were silent, each absorbed in his own thoughts, while collectively their hearts ached for the stranger riding with them. A blue grouse scuttled off, momentarily took flight, and then noisily crashed onto a low-drooping branch. Lane's horse, Tubbs, nervously sidestepped. "Easy, boy." Lane eased him back into line. The rest of the horses barely noticed.

Chris had spoken to the Chinook crew on his radio just before they set out on the trail. They had no news except that they had spotted a reflection not far from the intersection of the Purgatoire trail and the Trinchera trail, a critical juncture because the trails headed off in almost opposite directions from that point. A wrong turn could mean days of fruitless searching. They decided it might be John's jeep causing the reflection. His father, the general, had told them his son's name and that he was driving a 1990 Jeep Wrangler. The Chinook crew then headed back to Fort Carson because they had used up their allotment of fuel by loitering over the search site. The riders were on their own.

The trail brought them within earshot of the Purgatoire River, which was swollen with spring runoff. The roar of the rushing water soon rivaled that of the Chinook engines during take off.

For a few minutes, talking was hopeless. They climbed up and away from the river's banks, and the roar dimmed to a distant humming.

"Where did the river get the name Purgatoire?" The question was unexpected, and it interrupted the reverie. Of the group, only one did not know the story of the Purgatoire River. Steve was closest to the general, but it wasn't his place to speak out first among so many Cuchara natives. There was some kind of storytelling pecking order that he didn't quite understand but always respected. Chris had seniority when it came to telling outsiders about the local lore. Don had seniority for telling horse or hunting stories. Everyone waited for Chris to begin.

"Spanish explorers, accompanied by a group of priests, came to this region in the early 1700s. They may have been the very first Europeans. Their mission was to look for gold, and supposedly, they found a rich vein in the Spanish Peaks. They forced some of the local Indians to dig it out for them and then promptly killed 'em. The Spaniards then headed south over Cuchara Pass. They followed the river, hoping to cross the Sangre de Cristo range. They were attacked by another band of Indians—word traveled fast—and were slaughtered on the banks of the river. That's how the river got its name: Rio de las Animas Perdido en Purgatorio, since the Spaniards believed if they died without receiving last rites, they would descend into purgatory. The name was later changed to Purgatoire by French trappers."

Before the general could respond to the story, Don pulled up and stopped. There was room enough, so everyone eased their horse up next to Don for a better look.

A black Jeep Wrangler was parked just to the right of the trail. Its cloth top was littered with dry pine needles. Steve felt his stomach turn over. All the riders dismounted, and the general quick-stepped ahead of everyone. He reached into his pocket and pulled out a set of keys. The white Tennessee plates contrasted sharply against the black paint.

The general's hands shook as he inserted the key and opened the driver's side door. He sat in the seat and began rummaging through the debris on the dash and the floor. After a few harried moments, he slid out of the Jeep and addressed Chris in a trembling voice, "Maybe you ought to look. I don't know exactly what I'm looking for." Chris nodded to him and eased behind the steering wheel, methodically scanning every piece of paper he could find. Bill Peterson, another search member, opened the back window and began shuffling through the camping gear. Chris was hoping for a map of the area for any indication where John may have headed. Bill was pulling gear out of the back and spreading it on the ground. First a one-man tent, then a sleeping bag, a Coleman lantern, and finally a backpack. The general was turning it over and examining all of it. Apparently, John had left all of his camping gear in the Jeep. "Here's something," Chris said. He sounded very matter-of-factly, as if he could discharge some of the emotion beginning to run through the group. It was a section of a topographical map of Trinchera Peak and the adjacent trail system, including the one where they stood. They could see a circle drawn around Purgatoire Campground. Chris sat and just looked at the map for a few minutes. He spread it out on the hood of the Jeep and pointed to the campground. "Don, how long to hike over to the campground from here?"

"A strong hiker on a good day could do it in four to five hours," Don replied. "I don't get why he left his gear if he was planning to go all the way there. He couldn't possibly make it back before dark."

"General, do you have any ideas? Did John talk to you about his plans?" Chris needed the father to help them out. He was grasping for straws, any hints to point them in the right direction. They couldn't afford any wild goose chases.

"All he told me was he wanted to see Trinchera Peak and possibly four-wheel up to the peak if the trail was passable. He never mentioned Purgatoire Campground. In fact, I had the impression he wanted to really rough it, away from any other campers." The general was clearly frustrated.

"Maybe he tried to drive up to Trinchera and the trail was blocked. Remember, that was about eight days ago. He could have decided to hike over to Purgatoire but went to scout the trail before hauling all his gear out thinkin' he'd come back here to spend the night and get an early start the next day," Chris mused out loud to no one in particular.

"Or he could have just changed his mind and gone out to look for a good place to camp nearby," the general chimed in.

"What about footprints?" Steve asked almost apologetically. Don smiled and quipped, "I told you I needed him along." Of course, they had trampled the ground to a pulp in the immediate vicinity of the Jeep. Don got out his flashlight because the ground was shady. He began moving slowly along the trail toward Purgatoire, his eyes following the light beam. He walked until he was almost out of sight and then returned along the other side as if trying to will John's tracks to materialize.

"I can't say for sure, but there seem to be some impressions that could be boot prints. Chris, why don't we ride down to Elk Meadow? It's a fairly central location. We can look for other signs on the way. We'll camp there and get an early start in the morning. We're gonna run out of daylight before long."

Everyone agreed. The general had put his trust in these men and was grateful they had made a decision.

Steve's legs and butt ached as he stretched to remount Willie. He had never ridden so far this early in the summer and grimaced at the thought of a full day in the saddle tomorrow.

Only two of the riders really knew how to look for signs of John's passage, so they rode well in front of the main party, visually scouring the ground and nearby branches and bushes. They were looking for anything not natural to the environment—a piece of fabric, a candy wrapper, or some disturbance in the trail.

Thirty minutes of silent riding brought them to the outskirts of Elk Meadow (named for the annual gathering of one of the largest Elk herds in Colorado). Steve had been here twice before but was awestruck by the view as they left the cover of the pines and entered a magnificent outdoor cathedral. Trinchera Peak, at 13,517 feet, towered above them to their right with Teddy's Peak just beyond. The Culebra Range stretched out as far as the eye could see against the backdrop of the day's fading light. The mantle of snow draped around Trinchera's shoulders glistened in contrast to the alpine valley's spring greenery. The meadow was the width of two football fields and as long as three. It appeared to be fairly flat, but the riders could feel the earth's slope as they adjusted their positions in the saddle to compensate.

Steve could see the snow-filled bowl just below Trinchera's summit. It was a Cuchara tradition for a few of the locals to hike up to the bowl with ski gear and ski down on July the fourth. Occasionally, a tourist would want to make the trek for bragging rights. Naturally, the usual two-hour leisurely hike became a four-hour climb of agony when the "guide" took them the long way. By the time they were in position, the innocent interloper, unaccustomed to such strenuous exertion at high altitude, was so exhausted they could barely make it down on skis. The locals always had a good laugh, and the victim was too embarrassed to talk about it.

The riders congregated around Don, who was already out of his saddle, and began dismounting. Steve knew he had to hustle. He unsaddled Willie, leaving his bridle, and hurried to the general's horse. "I'll take him, sir," he said, sounding as authoritative as any awestruck fourteen-year-old could be when addressing a general. "Thanks, son." The general could have muddled through unsaddling his own horse, he felt sure, but the truth was, he was exhausted. And he didn't want to trample Steve's earnest enthusiasm.

Steve was in a race with the horses. Most of the other riders would unsaddle their own, but Steve wanted to avoid the equine mayhem he had witnessed on another pack trip. Michael, who usually handled all the horse chores on these trips, had "lollygagged" (Don's word) and allowed the saddled horses to wander off as they began to graze. The first thing the horses wanted to do after being ridden all day was to drop down to the ground and roll on their backs. Don was yelling at Michael as they both rushed around, coaxing the horses back onto their feet before they ruined their saddles or hurt themselves. Steve had wanted badly to help but didn't know what to do, so he stood helplessly and watched. This time, the horses were relieved of their saddles and tied up in a fairly straight line. Steve led one horse at a time away from the campsite, hobbled their front feet, and removed their bridles. They looked comical as they awkwardly jump-stepped around the meadow, raising and extending their front feet together to move from one grassy snack to another. This was a time-tested, benign method of keeping horses from wandering off while affording them mobility to graze and take water.

The saddles were arranged in a straight line with the saddle blankets spread on top to dry out. Before turning in, Steve would cover them with a tarp to protect them from the dew. Don had a couple of cook fires roaring and was busily preparing what they all knew would be one of the finest meals ever cooked outdoors. Don's cowboy cooking was legendary. It was all done in Dutch ovens and an iron skillet, and he could put most traditional chefs to shame.

Steve found a fairly smooth, level piece of ground to set up his one-man tent and spread his sleeping bag inside. He wouldn't presume to help the general with so simple a task; he had obviously pitched a tent before. Lane's tent was close by, and the other riders were finding their spots. The dogs were showing the wear and tear of the day. Bear had plopped down right in the middle of Don's kitchen and surveyed the camp activities. Sampson was rolling in the tall grass, snuffling and groaning. Darkness stole in quietly and covered the camp with a gentle solitude. With their stomachs full and grateful, and after helping Don clean up, the group gravitated to various sitting positions facing the campfire. The mood was quiet as sleep began stalking the camp.

Steve stood up and headed toward his tent. He looked around for Sampson and saw that he was approaching the general who was sitting on the ground leaning against the carcass of a fallen pine. Not wanting to call out to Sampson and disturb the camp, he headed that way, afraid Sampson would be an unwanted intrusion.

As he approached the pair, he saw Sampson sit as if by command and then watched the general extend his right hand toward Sampson, who responded by lifting his paw. The general wrapped his hand around the offered paw, shook it and petted Sampson on the head. His body language displayed his pleasure with Sampson's attention. He's a dog lover for sure, thought Steve. Don told him he could tell by the way a rider first approached a horse how they were going to get along. "The thing with horses," Don would say, "is that you have to establish who's in charge right away. If you're timid or unsure of yourself, they'll take charge and control the ride."

The general looked up as Steve approached. "I hope he's not bothering you, sir."

"No, not at all. What's his name?"

"Sampson."

"What a good strong name," the general said. "He even has curly hair, too."

Steve had indeed taken the name from the Bible story. He couldn't remember much of it, except that Sampson was the strongest man on earth and couldn't be defeated as long as his hair was long. He had killed a lion barehanded and killed a bunch of enemies (he supposed they had been God's enemies). Sampson was the only Bible story he could remember where the word "ass" was mentioned. He wondered, grinning at his own cleverness, if that meant that Sampson was a "holy bad ass." Steve squelched that line of amusement. His mom used to tell him that God, for sure, had a sense of humor. He just didn't know if it would extend to referring to a biblical warrior as a "bad ass."

Steve eased to the ground and sat. "Can I ask you a question?" he queried the general.

"Sure, what is it?"

"What were you general of?" Steve asked.

"When I retired, I was the commander of the air force's military airlift command at Scott Air Force Base in Illinois. We were responsible for maintaining the airlift capability of the air force. We flew the C-141 Starlifter and the C-5 Galaxy mostly. I've been retired for almost five years now."

"Do you miss the air force?"

"Oh, sure. I miss the flying part, but I keep real busy."

They sat in silence as the general took Sampson's head in both hands and rubbed his ears. "My son John has an English setter that he hunts with. He loves to take him out and work him."

Without thinking, Steve asked, "How old is John?"

"He's thirty-two years old. He's a real outdoorsman. A lot like you. His best friend and he had been planning this camping trip for a year. At the last minute, the friend had to cancel. John was determined to come to Colorado, so he came on by himself. It's not like him to take risks, especially when he's by himself." The general grew quiet and concentrated on Sampson's massive head.

"This is the best search-and-rescue team in southern Colorado," Steve offered.

"I can tell they're very professional. I feel very fortunate that they're here. And grateful," the general replied. He continued, "I'm used to always being in charge, so it's a little strange to have someone else making all the decisions."

"My dad was in the army. In Vietnam," Steve told him as if he had just remembered. "He was a member of the 101st."

"Well, I admire him greatly. That was a tough, tough place to be. I hope you never have to serve in a war like that," he said.

"Was John in the military?"

"No, the military never appealed to him. I suppose being a kid in a military family gave him a totally different view of the military life."

Steve thought that he should probably stop intruding, so he stood up and said, "I'd better be sacking out. Come on, Sampson."

"Good night, Steve, and thanks for the visit."

Steve and Sampson made their way to the tent. The campfire was reduced to a pile of coals but gave off a comfortable glow. Steve turned around and looked at the general.

He was just sitting. Watching, searching the darkness.

REUNITED AT PURGATOIRE

Steve crawled into his sleeping bag. Sampson stretched out so that his back was firm against Steve's body. Steve was asleep almost immediately. The next thing he knew, he was wandering in total darkness. Strange. He could have sworn that there had been moonlight when he went to bed. He seemed to be heading toward the Purgatoire River, which was roaring loudly. I'd better be careful, he thought, and not stumble into the water. Even though he couldn't see a thing, he walked confidently toward the growing din.

He could see the water now, a good five or six feet below him. It seemed to be creating its own light source, so he could easily see the other bank, at least ten feet away. Sampson was swimming in the roiling waters, but he was not making any progress against the powerful rush. Soon it occurred to Steve that Sampson was in trouble. Because of the steepness, neither bank afforded a place for him to exit the river nor could Steve reach him. Sampson looked up at him and barked, but there was no sound. Steve shouted but could not hear himself over the noise. He began to panic. He thought he should get Don's rope and tie one end around a tree with the other end around his waist and jump into the river. Maybe he could then pull both of them out of the water. He had to save Sampson! The rope was in his hands, but he could tell it was much too short to be of any use. He could see that Sampson was tiring. He watched Steve as if waiting for Steve to tell him what to do. The rushing water was relentless.

Steve looked around in desperation. He could see his mom standing on the opposite bank. She was speaking to him, but the words died as quickly as they left her expressionless face. Steve began crying. He didn't know what to do. "Mom, Mom," he screamed. "Please help me."

Nothing. She just watched.

Steve couldn't leave Sampson in the water by himself. He would jump in downriver of Sampson and grab him as the river swept him downstream. There would be a place to exit the river. There had to be. He jumped! The water was mind-numbingly cold, yet he was sweating profusely.

888888888888888

He opened his eyes. The smell of frying bacon, not freezing water, filled his nostrils. A hint of daylight peeked into his tent. Sampson stirred and then stretched the sleep from his body. Steve hurriedly dressed so he could help Don with breakfast and go check on the horses. He wanted to be out and about before the rest of the camp woke up. Images from his dream lingered but began to fade away as the morning brightened.

All of the men wanted to be on horseback at first light, so breakfast was a hurried affair. Steve had removed the hobbles from the horses and had them in position, waiting to be saddled. Their collective breath sent a cloud of frost into the chilled air.

Chris had the topographic map spread out on the ground. He was making suggestions about who should ride in what direction. Don pulled Steve aside.

"I think you should ride with John's father. I don't want you off by yourself and we need to make sure he doesn't get lost. Remember the trail we rode last summer to count bighorn sheep for the Department of Wildlife? Stay on it to the top of the ridge then ride back down following Cucharas Creek. We'll meet back here at noon and go from there."

Steve nodded. He suspected that Don was sending them out in the most unlikely direction to find John.

The two of them rode silently for the first half hour, content to listen to the labored breathing of their horses as they negotiated the steep trail. The morning sun dappled the forest floor where skittish chipmunks and ground squirrels hurried away.

"John! John!" the general shouted into the forest every few minutes. It gave him a sense of trying—a sense of doing *something*. Even if John couldn't respond, he might know that they were there, getting closer to him. Maybe it would comfort him. Both Steve and the general swept their eyes across the landscape in the hope of seeing some out-of-place sign.

About ten o'clock, they reached flat ground, and Steve thought it would be a good place to rest and water the horses.

"John would love living here," his father said.

"What kind of job does he have?"

"He's a structural engineer in Nashville. He helps design really big projects like stadiums, convention centers, and bridges. He makes sure they will stay up once they're built."

"Wow," Steve replied. "He must be really smart."

"Oh, he's smart all right. Although he doesn't always exercise his smartness. Like going on this trip,"

Steve didn't respond. He loved to be off by himself and often hiked for hours. That was one reason his dad had bought the puppy soon after they moved here. He always told someone where he was going.

"Does John have brothers or sisters?" Steve changed the subject.

"No, he's an only child."

The general continued with stories about John's boyhood and how hard it was for an air force brat to adjust to new schools, make new friends every couple of years. There was a note of regret as he remembered how much harder it had gotten for John with each of his father's promotions. The old saying "it flows downhill" also applied. As the rank piled up on the shoulders of a rapidly advancing officer, so did the advanced expectations "flow downhill" onto the unsuspecting shoulders of the officer's child. John was expected to behave appropriately and achieve suitably as an officer's son. He couldn't help wondering if John was still trying to meet his expectations and those of the air force as he gravitated toward somewhat extreme outdoor pursuits.

John had excelled at his engineering classes but not without personal costs. He needed to study so hard for all of his classes that he had abandoned any hope of a social life in college. His parting gift for graduating with honors from Vanderbilt University was a stomach ulcer. Steve learned that John had pursued his career with the same single-minded fervor that extended to his leisure.

"But he is the most likeable guy you'll ever meet, Steve," the general assured him. Steve desperately wanted to find out for himself.

Cucharas Creek was both their guide and their companion as they headed back down the steep hill. Its headwaters bubbled rather than burst from the mountainside. It oozed out of the ground, found the most direct way down, and was soon joined by enough snowmelt to gouge away the earth and establish a virtual freeway to the Purgatoire River.

Their gait changed appreciably as the horses worked to keep from tumbling headfirst down the mountain.

"Sir, I don't know if you've ever ridden down such a steep slope or not, but you should lean back a little in the saddle and ease your feet forward. Give the horse his head and let him pick his way down. That's easier for him to do if you loosen up on the reins," Steve instructed matter-of-factly over his shoulder.

"I understand, Steve. Thanks." The general hadn't heard such to-the-point, understandable, clear instructions since he had his first flying lesson at Moody Air Force Base almost forty years ago.

The terrain changed dramatically for the better once they crossed the Purgatoire River. Riding side by side, they could carry on a casual conversation without straining their necks or voices. It was just past noon and the sun had chased away the early-morning cold. It was a classic Colorado day crowned with a brilliant mountain sky.

Steve pulled up. He listened for a minute and started back up. He stopped again.

"Did you hear that?" He cocked his head in the direction they had been earlier.

"I think its Sampson," he whispered.

They sat quietly for a few minutes. There! It wasn't barking. Steve had never heard Sampson howl. He was sure, though, that Sampson was the source of the low mournful wail.

Steve felt a knot in his stomach. What if Sampson was injured? If he had surprised a black bear, he could be in big trouble. They headed up the mountain again, but without a trail. The aspen trees crowded them every way they turned. Steve was trying to think clearly. He knew they should be careful on this terrain. It would make things worse by magnitudes if one of them or a horse was injured. They reached a small clearing that leveled out, slightly allowing them to dismount. Steve yelled, "Sampson, Sampson. Come here, boy." Now he could hear Sampson barking—a determined, steady chorus, not casual because-I'm-a-dog-barking. Now, there's plaintive howling again.

"Sir, I've got to go find Sampson." Steve was torn. He felt some responsibility not to abandon the general who was somewhat in his care. Then there was his responsibility, though small, as a member of the search party.

The general made his own decision. "I'll go with you, Steve. You may need help."

They started up. Sampson provided them with an unwavering, lonely homing beacon. Soon they were both breathing heavily, but the general was suffering from the exertion at well over eleven thousand feet of elevation. They measured their progress not by distance traveled but by their closing proximity to Sampson's wailing.

It gave no warning—towering, ominous, silent, and waiting. A rock wall soared hundreds of feet. It was as if a galactic earthmover had swung its bucket and dug out tons of earth to create a vertical wall. The base looked to be about three hundred feet and rose straight up from the trees. They were standing about one-third of the way from its northernmost extension. The top (what they could see of it) extended in a wavy line with its highest point appearing to be a couple of hundred feet in elevation. The face looked like smooth, almost chiseled rock.

Sampson was close by. He had not let up, and Steve thought he was near the southern end of the rock face. They moved quickly as the ground was fairly level. Soon they could see where a large number of rocks had rolled through the woods, evidently with great force, knocking many trees to the ground. They were soon walking on a carpet of rocks and having to climb over fallen and crushed trees. There must have been a cataclysmic event to create this much destruction.

Sampson stood at the edge of the trees almost at the base of the rock wall.

He began barking excitedly when he saw Steve but stood his ground. Steve feared that he had been injured or was trapped. Sampson always, but always, came running to greet Steve.

"What is it, boy?" Steve approached him gingerly to keep him as calm as possible. Sampson finally stopped barking and howling and began whining. He was excited and fidgety and acted like he wanted to dig, but the rocks were too big.

The general had gotten very quiet. Steve looked over at him. He was staring at the rock wall. "I think John's here," he said softly.

Steve was stunned. "What makes you think that?"

"Something John said a couple of weeks ago about being anxious to learn rock climbing. He had been out with a couple of rock-climbing instructors and was really enthusiastic. I just never put this camping trip together with climbing." The general continued, "And Sampson definitely thinks something is under all that rock." His voice trailed off.

Steve had never considered Sampson to be part of the search effort. He had not been trained to track, nor had he been trained to locate avalanche victims. Steve was dumbfounded to think John might be buried here. They needed help badly. There were hundreds, thousands of rocks spread out over a wide area. Steve didn't know what to do. He felt overwhelmed. How were they going to contact the others? How could they possibly do this without more help?

The general knew exactly what to do and how to do it. "Steve, you've got to get on Willie and return to camp. The rest of the party will return there around noon. Tell them what we found and why I think John's here. I'll stay here and start removing rocks. We have no idea how deeply he may be buried or if is still alive, but we have to try," the general directed. He was on sure ground: assess the situation, determine the most logical course of action, understand the risks, and take action. Until he knew differently, he would assume that John was alive. This rock pile may not have been the most logical place to look for John, but Sampson was the wild card that convinced the general. He had built his thirty-year military career on using a combination of hard facts, suppositions, assumptions, intellect, advice, and intuition to make tough decisions. He wasn't a general for nothing.

"Steve!" the general called out. "Be careful. I'm counting on you."

Steve made sure the general's horse was securely tied and mounted Willie. He left Sampson with the general. Willie negotiated the steep terrain with no trouble and soon broke out of the trees onto more hospitable ground. Steve put Willie into an easy lope and headed back to camp. What if they weren't back yet? Should he build a signal fire? How he wished they all carried radios, but the meager budget for rescue work did not provide for that luxury. The volunteer medical crews (EMTs) carried radios, but their range was limited and they were passed around to those who were on call.

He could see horses tied up and felt a surge of relief. Someone was there!

They had seen Steve approaching and knew that something was wrong.

Steve began explaining as soon as he left the saddle. Willie was breathing hard, his sweaty sides heaving.

They discussed unemotionally the wisdom of dedicating all of their resources to one site given the scarcity of hard evidence of John's location, the probability of recovering a live victim versus a dead body from underneath such a massive rockslide, and the logistics of setting up a remote camp to sustain them for any length of time. Steve was glad that the general didn't have to overhear this very necessary yet callous-sounding planning. The general certainly would have understood and appreciated the thoroughness of the discussion, but the father would have agonized.

Don said he had enough food for two more days if everyone could subsist on beef jerky. Chris agreed that the chances of recovering John alive were next to zero, but they were all either someone's father or someone's son, and each of them privately pledged not to give up the fight.

"Steve, I need you to take Jebediah and some empty water containers back down to Cucharas Creek and fill 'em up. We'll have to pack in all the drinking water for us and the horses," Don instructed. "You can show us where you headed up the mountain side and then continue on to the creek."

Lane and Don both were a little concerned about Jebediah's behavior. The mule was the strongest, most able pack animal of the bunch, but he could be very ornery and amazingly stubborn at times. Don tied Jebediah's lead rope to Willie's saddle horn. Willie had worked cattle for years and had ridden in rodeos all over Colorado. He had ridden full speed next to bucking bareback broncs, saddle broncs, and even 1,800-pound bulls, providing an escape route for their riders when the eight-second buzzer sounded. He was used to being bumped by other animals, many of whom were highly agitated, and to bumping back when necessary. Willie knew how to keep his cool. He had been trained to take care of his rider.

Don loaded the rest of his gear onto the other pack mule, and the men were soon saddled up and were on their way. Steve pointed the way for them at the cutoff. He continued on to Cucharas Creek as the other riders turned up the mountain to find the rockslide.

Sampson greeted them at the edge of the rock field, barking. They found the general near exhaustion, bent over with a rock, much too big for one man, cupped in his arms.

They eased it out of his arms and escorted him over to a grassy area.

Chris sat him down. "General, listen. I've done a lot of search-and-rescue missions. The number one rule is that the rescuers have to take care of themselves before they can rescue anybody. If you collapse from exhaustion, break a leg, or fall over dead, you can't help us find John, plus we gotta carry you out. Think about it. Now I want you to rest here while we get set up."

The general nodded. All he needed to hear was an authoritative voice speaking with logic and facts and he could allow himself to rest. He was near exhaustion.

Chris didn't quite know how to react to Sampson's behavior. He had worked with trained avalanche dogs before, but they reacted with a very specific, trained response when they encountered a buried victim's scent. He had also attended training with cadaver dogs. Could Sampson instinctively have recognized that a victim (or a body) was buried here? He did know one thing for sure: it was all they had. Sampson had not left the spot since Steve first found him. He had quieted down, but he continued to linger around the spot as if supervising their work.

The men defined a circle from which they would remove rocks. They established a "dumping ground" down-slope from their search area and set up an assembly line so they could move the heavier rocks out of the circle efficiently and get them out of the way. They would each rotate to a new position every fifteen minutes, either picking rocks out of the growing hole or moving the larger rocks along to the newly formed pile. They simply flung the smaller rocks out of the way but always in the same predetermined direction so no one would be injured.

The general, watching them spring into action with such resolute precision, began to weep. He was so tired, so glad to see them, so relieved to ease some of his burden onto their able shoulders, and so moved by their heroic efforts on his and John's behalf.

Jebediah behaved beautifully. Steve dismounted Willie and tied up both animals near the other horses so they could graze. He unsaddled Willie and the other horses. The other riders had left in a hurry, leaving these chores for Steve. He knew they would be here for the night. Using some of his precious cargo, he watered the horses. He had watered Willie and Jebediah at the creek, so they were okay. Now, he just had to coax the mule the rest of the way up the hill. If he could just get him moving and keep him moving, he should be okay. He knew that Jebediah was strong and surefooted enough to do it. The question was, did he *want* to do it?

Lane was greatly relieved when Steve showed up with the mule and the water all in one piece. He interrupted his backbreaking routine to come over and greet Steve.

"Everything go okay?" He slipped his arm around Steve's shoulders.

"Yeah, Dad. Poor Willie is worn out, but everything went just fine. Any signs of John?" he asked reluctantly.

"No. Nothing. Go get yourself some jerky. We're going to keep working and just take short breaks for food and water."

"Okay. I just need to get Jebediah tied up for the night," Steve replied. He was amazed at how much rock they had moved. They were now standing in a sizeable depression.

Don was glad to see Steve also. Steve reported on the status of the horses and Jebediah. "Good man, Steve. We're gonna need a couple of bonfires so we can keep workin' after dark. One over there and one about here," Don gestured to his chosen spots. "If you would, also start a cook fire so we can brew some coffee." The jerky would have to wait.

Steve alternated between throwing firewood on the roaring fires and digging out rocks with his bare hands. They worked in a frenzied monotony as Sampson stood guard over the surreal scene. The men and their shadows seemed intertwined in a bizarre dance between the leaping flames.

They found John's body at 1:30 a.m. They asked his father to please stand aside while they delicately removed the last rocks from his mountain cairn. Chris cradled John's head as they gently lifted him out. Freed at last from his rock tomb, John lay peacefully at rest. The general kneeled at the side of his only, and now lost, son. The rest of the men moved away in silent despair. Lane put his arm around Steve's shoulders as his son sobbed uncontrollably. Steve leaned into his dad.

The night air was biting cold. The men began to unroll their sleeping bags but had few hopes of sleep. Steve took his and the general's sleeping bag over to him. He put his hand on the grieving father's shoulder. The general slumped into a sitting position and buried his face in his hands and sobbed. Steve draped the sleeping bag over the general's shoulders and sat on the ground next to him. Sampson sidled up to the general and laid his big curly head in his lap.

The three of them kept vigil over John during his last night on the mountain. Steve slept fitfully, leaning against the general. The only time he got up, he saw his mom watching them. He wanted desperately to go and explain to her what was happening and to see if she was coming home, but he couldn't move. He called to her, but his voice died as quickly as he spoke. He could see that she was crying. For him? For the dead son? For herself? For his dad? A part of him remembered she was dead, but his dream self still believed that if he could reach her, she would come home. She reached out as if to touch him, to comfort him. He could see it in her face now. Her tears were gone and she was smiling. Her hand touched him.

"Steve, we need to break camp." Lane was gently squeezing Steve's arm. Steve nodded and got up slowly. Chris was bending down next to the general and speaking softly. Chris rose and pulled the general up with him. They needed to prepare John's body for the trip back. Chris had brought a coroner's body bag. Several of them worked quickly and efficiently. Don had built a travois out of pine saplings and boughs to transport John. Don would pull him since he was the most experienced horseman.

The general told them John would be mighty proud to be carried off the mountain in such style by the finest group of men and dogs he had ever known.

Men, dogs, and horses were a haggard lot when they finally reached the trailhead at Blue Lake Campground. They were bone weary, beaten down by their journey. Chris drove down the mountain to a phone and called the Huerfano County coroner while Don trailered the horses. Chris took care of the required notifications to the county and state. The general made his personal phone calls. Fort Carson would send a helicopter to transport him and John to Peterson AFB in Colorado Springs, where they would meet an air force plane for their final trip home.

When it came time to say goodbye, the general embraced each of the men silently. He hugged Steve a little bit longer and promised him that yes he would come back to visit him under better circumstances.

A couple of nights later, still a little bruised by their ordeal, Steve and Lane sat by their fireplace. Sampson was stretched out on the floor, his sleep occasionally punctuated with a twitching leg.

"I wonder if dogs really do dream or if all that twitching is just muscle contractions." Lane mused.

Steve watched Sampson for a minute before replying. "Dad, I dreamed about Mom."

Lane was silent, looking for an answer in the fire. "I dream about her too, Steve. In fact, I think about her a lot." He paused for a minute. "I miss your mom terribly. Would you tell me about your dream?"

THE HOMESTEAD

The rest of the summer passed uneventfully and all too quickly for Steve. His and Lane's new school year started on the same day. Lane relished the intellectual give-and-take of the classroom, the first-day anticipation of the students, and the frenetic atmosphere of the first few days back on campus. The campus was much smaller than what he was used to, but it was comfortable and pleasant. The buildings were thirty years old and very institutional and drab, but the campus was in sight of the Wet Mountains to the west. Lane's office was in the business building, even though the course he taught was a combination of political science and strategic management. The business dean and the university president had already scheduled him to conduct seminars for a group of CEOs in Colorado Springs and for the governor and several key state legislators in Denver. His life was slowly but surely beginning to feel normal.

As Lane and Steve began to feel at home in Cuchara, Lane began toying with the idea of moving into the family homestead. It hadn't been lived in for over twenty years and would need a complete restoration. Steve was all for it. He relished the idea of having over 150 acres all his own—with a river running through it to boot. Plus, it was closer to LaVeta.

They took Chris with them for their first up-close look. He had a very practical streak and was a skilled carpenter. The original rock house was over one hundred years old, built by Sven Curry, an immigrant from Sweden. The family lore was that he had met and married his wife his first day in the valley and then changed his last name to better fit in his new country. He and his bride built the house and the array of rock walls. Over the years, they and subsequent family members had added three barns, all very sturdy and still serviceable. Steve couldn't resist imagining his own horse grazing by the Cucharas River, which coursed through the Curry property.

The house was a mess. The bottom floor, much like a basement with a walkout, had been used to house some type of small farm animals and was covered with decades—old dung. The septic tank had rusted out, the plumbing was shot, the electrical wiring needed replacing, and there were no closets. The main floor had wood flooring, which could be restored, but there were no cabinets in the small kitchen. The attic was large enough for a bed, but not much else. The interior walls were solid and intact. Sven had apparently been thinking long term when he laid the foundation because it was solid rock.

"What do you think, Chris?" Lane asked.

"I think we can have it livable in six months," Chris replied. "You and Steve get busy cleaning, and I'll start the materials list so we can price it out."

Lane looked at Steve who was carrying an armful of debris out the front door. Somehow Lane had the impression that the decision had already been made.

Cuchara's first real snowstorm of the season almost always barrels down the valley at Halloween. By then, the Curry homestead had been scrubbed clean and Chris and his on-again-off-again crew had done wonders to the interior. Electricity was just around the corner. The new septic tank had been installed with a new leach field. Chris had convinced Lane to drill a new, deeper water well. The existing water supply came from a shallow spring that yielded questionable drinking water due to migrating ground water pollution from the hundreds of ancient metal septic tanks in and around Cuchara. Lane had opted to use wood heat only, at least for the first winter. Steve would take the "basement," so Chris put in a separate bathroom and a smaller wood stove for him. Lane wanted only enough room for a bed and a comfortable chair for reading, so he took the attic. Since Chris was replacing the roof anyway, he installed a couple of dormers to open up the attic and bring in more light.

Steve and Lane had put in hours and hours, not only cleaning, but performing menial labor for Chris so that he could concentrate on the more skilled remodeling tasks. As they neared the end, they all felt a new kinship in bringing back to life the family home whose history embodied the Curry family's very first days in the valley.

They moved in during spring break. Even though it was the last week in March, they got pounded by heavy snow and had to take a day off. Chris had his front-end loader out before sunrise the next day and cleared their new drive way. Sampson loved the fresh wet snow and romped through the high drifts with abandon. They moved the last of the household items into the Curry house just after five. Lane had the wood stove crackling with split aspen logs, and it was creating a virtual heat wave in the small house. All three of them—Steve, Lane, and Chris—shed their heavy coats and boots in the small covered-porch entrance. Lane handed Chris a freshly opened beer, and they toasted their first night in their new home.

THE VILLAGE

Each day, Lane and Steve slowly weaved their lives into the rhythms of Cuchara. Steve caught the school bus into LaVeta at the end of their driveway. Lane drove to the university twice a week and spent the rest of the week at his improvised resort office. They had discovered the best-kept dining secret in the Rocky Mountains was in Cuchara. The Timbers restaurant, which was operated by Joe and Ernie, attracted diners from as far away as Denver. The restaurant was warm and inviting and almost always packed. Diners entered into a central sitting area dominated by a large see-through fireplace. Even waiting was a social event, as Joe circulated among the customers and either met them for the first time or greeted old friends. Customers were guided either right or left into one of the two dining areas. The lucky ones shared the left side with the musician of the evening. It was the social hub of Cuchara during the peak summer season. Lane and Steve became faithful customers of the Timbers, where the extended family of Joe and Ernie soon adopted them as their own.

For less-formal dining or more-formal drinking, Lane wandered (nobody just walked in the village, they wandered or meandered) down the street to the Dog Bar. It was officially the Boardwalk Saloon but was traditionally known as the Dog Bar because all of the village dogs wandered in and out to greet the patrons and to beg for handouts. The music was louder and the drinking was harder. Weekend evenings sometimes became raucous as the local drinkers mixed with the golfers from LaVeta or the city slickers on vacation. More than once, the county deputy sheriff had to be invited up to sort out the customers. Those were few and far-between though. The Dog Bar was mostly inhabited by congenial drinkers on good terms with the world.

The one and only street in Cuchara was picturesque and lined with giant pine trees. A delightful mix of small businesses shared the commerce with the Timbers and the Dog Bar. The Country Store carried mostly grocery items but had an entrance into the adjacent gift shop which was adjacent to Cuchara Liquor. All shared the wooden boardwalk with the Dog Bar. Across the gravel street was the Timbers and the Cuchara Inn and an eclectic mix of real estate offices, retail shops, and coffee shops.

Since moving into their new house at the ranch, the two of them had become much more visible and known to the locals. They were not considered locals by any stretch, but given their family's history in the valley, they were not considered outsiders either.

Lane walked into the Timbers even though it was only 8:00 a.m. and they did not open until 11:00. Joe and Ernie always had hot coffee made as they began to plan the day, and they graciously shared their coffee and conversation with friend and stranger alike. Lane had become a regular early-morning guest. Steve sometimes liked to sleep in on Saturday, but since school had just let out for the summer, he was wired, and he tagged along with Lane for something to do. Lane was sitting in front of the Timbers with his first cup of the morning, wondering where Steve could have gone. He then saw him exit the end of the Timbers building. He had never noticed a door there.

"Dad, come here. This is really neat!" Steve waved his hand.

Lane got up, mostly out of curiosity, and walked up the boardwalk toward Steve. There was a small enclave in the building that was separated from the restaurant by a wall. Steve disappeared again and Lane followed him into what turned out to be a painting studio. The interior opened up to a high ceiling. The rear wall consisted of large windows, which flooded the room with morning light. Three easels, all burdened with huge canvasses, dominated the floor space. Stacks of paintings, some still in progress, leaned against every wall. Finally, his gaze found the center of this artistic throng—a very attractive brunette with a slight frame, clad in jeans and a flannel shirt, large gold earrings swinging in rhythm with the paint brush she was waving as she talked to Steve.

"Look, Dad. Isn't this a great painting?" Steve asked.

Lane moved toward them as he replied to Steve while staring at this animated, captivating art creature.

The canvas of Steve's admiration was six feet tall and five feet wide. The viewer stood face-to-face with five horses galloping full speed across a river and seemingly poised to charge right into the room. Lane could almost feel the water splashing from their hooves as they thundered across the river bottom.

"I'll say. It's a fantastic painting. By the way, my name is Lane Curry," he offered his hand to the artist. "I guess you've already met Steve. At least I hope he introduced himself."

"Yes, he did. I'm very impressed with his manners. I'm Mary." She took Lane's hand and shook it firmly. Lane noticed her blue eyes as they scanned his face for a split second. He moved across the room as another large painting caught his eye. A group of three riders, all of whom were dressed in buckskins, were crossing a river at full gallop. The lead rider seemed to be staring right through Lane. His fur cap was pulled down tight on his head of flowing black hair. His beard was splattered with traces of ice as the river spray had frozen on his face. His breath, like that of his horse, hung frostily in the cold mountain air. Two of the riders, one on each side and slightly behind, were looking back as if they were being pursued. Lane thought that he recognized a geographical feature in the background and was about to ask when Mary spoke up, "That's the Gap, minus the two houses and the fence, of course. And without the highway." She was standing right next to him, and Lane could hear her breathing almost in sync with his own.

The Gap

"You really have a way with horses. I can't believe how real they look." He pulled closer to the painting, almost as if to confirm the horses existed only on canvas.

"I love horses; their strength and grace are inspiring. I could paint them all day, but I have to pay the bills so I also do commissions. Like this." Mary walked to one of the easels with a partially finished canvas. It was a family portrait with two big Labrador retrievers frolicking with children. The images were only partially finished and looked ghostly against the vibrant colors of the background.

"Families who vacation or have cabins here love to have portraits painted at their favorite Cuchara spot. I get a lot of business that way. My passion, though, is painting the local landscape and wildlife, usually in historic terms, like this one. The riders are clearly in flight, fearful of someone or something chasing them. Who knows who or what. But life in early Cuchara was very hard and often dangerous."

Lane and Steve learned that Mary had lived in Cuchara for ten years and lived by herself in a small cabin next to Dodgeton Creek not far from the village. They left with an offer from Mary to give Steve art lessons.

Early summer meant mud in Cuchara. The snow melted grudgingly, refreezing at night and swelling the creeks and rivers during the day. Lane was watching the torrent of melted snow running through his back yard and trying to figure out how to redirect it to the lower meadow. He saw and heard the mud-spattered pickup sliding up his driveway just as Sampson bolted, barking, toward the offending noise. Like most ranch trucks, this one transported a blue heeler who acted as if he lived in the truck. This dog, instead of riding in the truck bed, was perched precariously on top of the cab. He ignored Sampson, who was dancing around the truck and barking furiously at these noisy strangers. Lane called him down, and Sampson retreated to the apple tree where he plopped down to watch, ready to spring into action at the first hint of danger.

Lane recognized the driver. He was Earl Wilson, the eighty-year-old patriarch of the valley's largest ranching operation and one of the county's wealthiest men. You couldn't tell from his appearance or from his demeanor though. His hat was as weathered as his face, frayed by years of hard outdoor work. His battered boots seemed to hold up a pair of worn and ragged jeans.

Lane stepped forward. "I'm Lane Curry, Earl. We haven't met, but I know who you are." He extended his hand, and Earl grabbed it and shook firmly.

"Nice to meet you, Lane. I'm really glad to see this place brought back to life. I knew your grandfather and, of course, your father too. They were really good folks." Earl's face, lined with age and sun, radiated kindness as he smiled at Lane. Lane trusted him instantly. His grip, though hard as a vise, was warm and welcoming.

"I have a business proposition for you." Earl got right to the point. "I want to lease your grass this summer. I'd pay you the going rate and would put about sixty cows up here. With all the snow we've had this winter, this place could probably support as many as seventy-five, but I've always been more conservative with my own grass and others'. I'll pay you for the seventy-five cows so you don't feel like you could do better."

Earl's reputation was usually described with terms like tough as nails, honest to a fault, best cattleman in the state, no nonsense. Lane didn't know the going rate for grass but suspected Earl knew it to the cent, and he couldn't imagine anybody he would rather do business with. He would welcome the extra income because the renovation had cost more than he had planned, and deep down, he relished the idea of the family property becoming productive again—the old-fashioned way.

"I look forward to doing business with you, Earl." Lane extended his hand, knowing that this was the only contract he would ever see, or need.

Steve had wandered out and was petting Earl's dog, Rebel, who was lounging on top of Earl's cab. Sampson was beside himself but behaved. Earl introduced himself to Steve.

"Did you ever hear the story of Jumper?" Earl asked Steve.

"No, who was Jumper?"

"Your great-grandfather used to run quite a cattle operation on this place. When his son, your grandfather, was about your age, they owned a Border collie named Jumper. Jumper made quite a name for himself."

Earl leaned against his truck and shifted his body weight to get comfortable. His demeanor changed, and his eyes seemed to be looking at some point in the distance that Lane couldn't quite see.

JUMPER

Jumper saw the big mama cow and her frisky calf out of the corner of her eye. They had wandered away from the herd, and Jumper knew she had to herd them back before they wandered too far. She wheeled around and ran full speed at the mama cow. All she had to do was get the mama moving in the right direction and the calf would follow. Jumper circled around to cut off her escape. Crouched low to the ground, Jumper eyed the big cow's sharp hooves. The mama, very protective of her calf, did not turn like she was supposed to but lowered her head and unexpectedly charged. Jumper scrambled wildly to avoid the thundering hooves. Sharp horns slashed and narrowly missed her scooting flank.

"Bear, round up!" bellowed Master. A gray flash of lightning streaked between Jumper and the charging, bellowing cow. Bear growled and snapped at the mama's slobbery nose, and the cow meekly turned and trotted back toward the herd with her calf bawling after her. All of the cows and their calves were soon safely in the pen.

Jumper was humiliated. Once again, Bear, Master's Australian shepherd, had to rescue Jumper and correct her mistake. Master had brought Jumper, a beautiful black-and-white Border collie, home as a pup to train as Bear's replacement. Jumper had the genes and the instincts to be a great herder, but she sometimes misread the cattle. Jumper did not understand all of this, but she knew when she did not do her job. Border collies are bred to work and are one of the most intelligent breeds.

"That's all right, Jumper," Boy consoled as he patted her head. Even though Boy was only ten years old, he helped his dad with all the chores on this big ranch. Boy's own mama had died. That meant that Boy and Master had to work extra hard to keep the ranch working smoothly. Jumper and Boy had developed that special bond reserved just for dogs and boys. But Jumper knew that Master was a hard man who did not tolerate animals that could not earn their keep. She also knew Boy had to defend her to Master, and that made her feel even worse.

As the snow began melting in the high country, many of the ranchers in the Cuchara Valley herded their cattle to high, lush pastures where the cattle would graze and grow fat during the short summer. Bear was one of the very best of the working breed that was so indispensable to the ranchers. He was fearless and knew exactly where Master wanted the cattle. He had even saved Master's life.

Master and Bear were up in the high country one September evening rounding up strays. Master's horse, Willie, had stumbled. Master had dismounted to check Willie's leg when a bull, grown half wild during the summer, charged Master. His sharp horns would surely have killed or seriously injured Master. Bear tore into the bull's path, grabbing the bull's slobbery nose between his teeth. Bear would not let go even though he was being dragged inches from the thundering hooves. The pain of Bear's teeth in his tender nose soon distracted the bull and he stopped, his hot breath heaving in and out past Bear's viselike grip. The bull was now more interested in this furry set of sharp teeth and stood perfectly still. Bear didn't give an inch. Master, now back on Willie, called Bear several times before he released the bull and began barking and snapping at the bull's feet. The cantankerous bull had had enough of this demon dog and trotted off. How could Jumper ever replace Bear?

The next morning was typical for Colorado in the spring. The air was crisp and cold and the blue sky shone brilliantly. When he had finished his chores for the day, Boy decided to ride Tubbs, the senior citizen of the ranch, up Cottonwood Canyon to check on the beaver dam.

"Jumper, let's go!" Boy called.

Soon Tubbs was saddled and they were off. Tubbs had been retired after many years of distinguished rodeo performances and, most lately, trail rides and roundups. His eyesight was failing, and Boy took extra care to pay him special attention. Jumper forgot her sadness of the day before and ran ahead with exuberance. As they approached the old wooden bridge over the Cucharas River, Boy dismounted and took Tubbs' reins. Boy was afraid Tubbs could no longer see well enough to avoid the holes in the aging timbers. The river was full of early spring runoff, and it roared like a freight train beneath them as they gingerly crossed the old bridge.

After a couple of hours of slow but steady climbing, Boy dismounted to give Tubbs a rest and to eat a late lunch. There was still a thick, heavy layer of snow on the ground, sheltered from the melting sun by towering pines and firs. Boy decided the going was getting too hard and didn't want to tire Tubbs, so he turned them around and headed back down the narrow trail.

Colorado is famous for unpredictable and fast-changing spring weather, especially at higher altitudes. One minute a bright sun cast shadows across the snowy path, and the next, a gray pallor enveloped the entire mountain. Fat snowflakes soon filled the air, and the temperature began to plummet.

All of a sudden, a doe darted from the brush, undoubtedly to distract them from her fawn's hiding place. Startled, Tubbs reared up on his hind legs and launched Boy into flight. It was over in a second. Tubbs bolted down the trail and narrowly missed trampling Jumper as she scampered out of his way.

Jumper clawed her way out of the snow bank and back up the trail. Boy lay quite and still.

Tubbs was about a hundred yards down the trail, his reins caught in the limbs of a fallen tree. Jumper panicked. The snow was falling faster now and visibility was getting worse, closing in like a shroud. She barked excitedly at Boy, but he did not budge. Why didn't he get up? What was wrong? After a few frenzied minutes, Jumper calmed down and began licking Boy's face. She licked and licked until he finally opened his eyes and began to move about. Jumper barked in relief. Boy looked at Jumper but did not get up to take charge of things.

Jumper tore down the trail to where Tubbs was patiently waiting, unaware of the danger. As Jumper approached, Tubbs began fidgeting and pulling on his reins. Jumper stopped and let Tubbs settle down. She then crouched on her belly and slowly moved toward Tubbs. When she reached him, she saw how his reins were tangled. She slowly began working at the reins, careful not to startle him. Finally, she freed the reins and gripped them in her mouth. The snow was accumulating quickly now, and Jumper sensed the fading light. After a slow climb, she carefully led Tubbs past Boy, who was almost covered in snow. Jumper dropped the reins and crept between Tubbs's huge feet. She knew that Tubbs could hurt her and Boy very badly if he were startled and unintentionally stepped on them.

Jumper had to act fast. She tugged and tugged on Boy's jacket. She did not dare bark because she might spook Tubbs. Finally, Boy began to move and reached out and grabbed Tubbs' tail to pull himself up. Thankfully, Tubbs barely seemed to notice. Jumper threaded her way between Tubbs's legs again and took the reins in her mouth. She slowly led Tubbs down the trail. After he began moving, Jumper eased up enough to let Tubbs find his own way.

Tubbs instinctively headed for home.

When they reached the old wooden bridge, Jumper hesitated. In the fading light, she inched out slowly ahead of Tubbs, leading him and digging through the snow to make sure the way was safe. She did this all the way across the bridge until they were safe on the other side. She constantly looked back to make sure Boy was still there, hanging on to Tubbs's tail.

Jumper could see light from the swinging lanterns through the falling snow and near darkness. She heard Master's voice booming, "Look there! I see them!"

Soon Master and the search-and-rescue crew surrounded them. She gladly and tiredly surrendered Tubbs's reins to Master.

Later, after Boy had been checked, after Tubbs had been put up in the barn with a nice helping of sweet feed, and after the rescue crew had bragged on Jumper and her heroic efforts, Master sat in front of the big wood stove and held Jumper in his lap for a long, long time.

THE CATTLE DRIVE

The McAfees, tourists on their first trip to Cuchara, had left Colorado Springs at 7:00 a.m. sharp so they could reach their rented cabin early in the day. Like most visiting drivers on Highway 12, Bob, the father, was distracted by one colorful vista after another, all framed by the radiant blue sky. When he rounded the curve at Devil's Backbone, he was traveling a modest thirty-five miles per hour, but he slammed on his brakes in surprise.

"What in the world?" he sputtered.

Highway 12 was covered with cattle! Horseback riders were scattered behind and in front of the herd, moving nonchalantly among the bellowing cows. One of the riders motioned Bob forward and eased his horse into the herd, creating a small avenue. Bob slowly inched forward, and the cows parted, a red-and-white sea of livestock. His two sons, aged seven and nine, were going wild with excitement. Creeping along, Bob exited the moving mass and saw that another rider up ahead had stopped a car from the opposite direction to wait for Bob to clear. As he slowly drove past the cowboy, the rider gave him a friendly wave. Bob glanced in the rearview mirror at the plodding herd. A boyhood memory of hundreds of stampeding cattle and furiously riding cowboys trying to turn the herd before it crashed from the movie screen flashed before him.

City slickers from Colorado Springs or Denver and flatlanders from Texas, Oklahoma, or Kansas were usually dumbfounded the first time they saw a cattle drive on Highway 12. Early in the summer, ranchers usually moved cattle up the mountain to high-grazing pastures and then moved them back down again in early fall. If you owned property along the highway and didn't want them wandering through your yard, it was your responsibility to put up a fence. Colorado was open-range country, and the cattle had the right of way.

The herd passed by the Curry "ranch" midmorning. Steve and Sampson were out in force, for they had heard the bellowing several miles away. Lane was out too, excited to begin this new chapter of their new life on the old family homestead. A rider had positioned himself on the highway just above the gate to their property to funnel the herd onto their driveway. Another rider was further up the road to stop traffic until they got all the stragglers in and the gate closed.

Sampson was tied up. They couldn't risk him running into the herd and spooking them. He was fidgeting and whining and occasionally barking at the intruders. He would have to get used to these strange creatures so he wouldn't chase them around the pasture.

Soon the guests were all in, the gate was closed behind them, and the riders were dismounting. Steve untied Sampson but held onto the leash. Earl had suggested they walk Sampson around the cattle and let him get used to their scent.

"He's a smart dog. He'll figure them out pretty quick."

Steve let the leash out as Sampson strained.

"Easy, boy," Steve said.

The cattle ignored him as he sniffed at their heels. As long as he wasn't nipping at them, they could care less. Steve unhooked the leash and let Sampson roam free among the herd. The patriarch of the herd, a Hereford bull named Leroy, ambled over to check out Sampson. Leroy was huge even by bull standards and sported a set of sharp horns. He was the "baddest" guy on this new block, and he was exerting his dominance, not only over his harem but over everyone else. Sampson got a little too close for Leroy's comfort, and he charged Sampson with his head down, scattering cattle to both sides. Sampson deftly dodged the menacing horns and scampered out of the way. As soon as Sampson regained his balance, he set his feet and lowered his ears. He was obviously going to make a stand. Steve could hear a low, guttural growl and saw Sampson's lip curl up, baring his teeth. He was about to intervene when Leroy decided he didn't want to fool with this furry distraction any longer. The bull bellowed as he shook his head furiously from side to side, slinging slobber all over Sampson before returning to his herd.

One of Earl's hands had pulled empty horse trailers so they could trailer their horses back down the highway. Steve noticed they were unloading one of them. Earl led a big gelding over to Steve and Lane. It was Willie.

"Don Emmons retired Willie after last season. He was beginning to develop arthritis and is getting on in age. Did you know Willie was a champion cutting horse before he retired to carry tourists around? Looks like he's retiring again. I don't really need another working horse, but I wanted to keep Willie in the valley. Would you mind looking after him? He does need to be ridden every so often, and you might want to give him some alfalfa hay during the winter to help him stay warm."

Steve couldn't believe his luck. Willie had become his favorite horse while working for Don. He had also developed a special bond with him during their search-and-rescue outing last year.

"Dad, I'll do it," Steve blurted out.

Lane could see that one of the hands had already unloaded Willie's saddle and tack. There was not much discussion about the matter.

"That's really generous of you, Earl." Lane looked at Earl.

"Well, there couldn't be a better place for an old work horse like Willie than to be with a young kid who loves him. And there's no better way to teach a boy about responsibility than to put him in charge of a horse. They make a good pair." Earl's eyes twinkled.

BRIGHT AND EARLY

The Curry herd of cattle settled into their daily routine with ease. Leroy was the undisputed master of his domain, and Willie was the most pampered steed in the valley. Lane had cleaned out all the barns except for his favorite one, the one they planned to use for Willie when the weather turned really cold. It was the largest and sturdiest, with an attic for hay storage, three stalls, and a single open area on the ground floor. A large wooden sliding door provided the only entrance on the ground level. The weathered, gray planks were still solid, and the metal roof, though spotted with rust, seemed to be in good shape. Lane had saved this job for last because it looked so nasty. There was a large pile of junk heaped into one of the long-unused stalls. It was the stall farthest from the door, and consequently, it was bathed in perpetual shadow. It gave Lane the creeps to rummage around in the near dark. It turned out most of the material was discarded and rotten clothing—shirts, aprons, and work pants, which Lane quickly threw into a large pile outside. A large trunk remained. Lane was able to scoot it a few inches at a time, first pulling on an old leather handle then pushing it ahead of him. He was breathing heavily by the time he got it outside in the light.

Musty old air greeted him when he pried the lid open. Numerous small rodents had obviously used the trunk over the years, bringing in straw and scrap material for nests. Lane removed the top layer of debris, mostly old dishes and eating utensils. The only interesting-looking piece was the size of a large coffee can. In fact, as Lane pulled it out, he could see that it *was* a coffee can—a Bright and Early Coffee can, a product of Duncan Coffee Co. The focal points of its design were a large rooster and once-bright red lettering. Lane remembered exactly where he had seen this can, or one just like it, when he was a small boy. His grandfather had taken him camping at Chaparral Falls. They had hiked up the Cottonwood Canyon Trail, which for some reason was a magical-sounding name to a young boy who had never spent the night outdoors. As his grandfather packed their supplies, he scooped coffee out of a Bright and Early can into a white cloth bag. The next morning, Lane had waked to a wonderland of fresh snow, a roaring cook fire, and the aroma of brewing coffee. It had been the very best day of his young life. Not long after the young Lane had returned home to Texas, his grandfather had died. He had not seen a Bright and Early can since then, but it was as clear to him today as it was on that cold Colorado morning almost thirty-five years ago. He took the can inside the house, cleaned it thoroughly, and looked for the perfect place to display the rusty family heirloom.

It was almost two weeks later when he was sitting on his front porch drinking a steaming cup of coffee and waiting for the sun to come up that he had his own bright and early idea. He was usually able to think more clearly before the day's activities cluttered his mind. This was Lane's favorite time of the day, the sun chasing away the cold of the night as it slowly overcame the darkness.

He was in Cuchara by 9:00 a.m., first checking out the Country Store and buying two cups of coffee, then sticking his head in the Timbers to see if Joe was up and about. He stepped out onto the boardwalk where he stood for a moment, apparently undecided about where to go next, then almost too nonchalantly strolled in the direction of the studio. The door was standing open and all the lights were on.

"Mary? Are you here?" Lane stuck his head through the open door but didn't step in. Mary stuck her head out from behind a large canvas.

"Come in."

Lane stepped into the studio. "Here, I thought you might like a fresh cup of coffee, but I bought it at the Country Store so I can't vouch for the fresh part."

"Well, as long as it's hot, I can overlook everything else. Thank you. What are you doing up here so early?"

"I might have a commission for you," he blurted out. He was second-guessing his bright idea now that it was time to tell Mary about it. He pulled the Bright and Early can out of a paper bag.

"I've got an idea for a painting of this coffee can."

Mary reached out, and he handed it to her. "So, are you thinking about a still life painting?" She turned the can around and inspected it.

"Sort of, but not a traditional still life."

"Oh yeah? I'm getting interested." She beamed at him.

That was a shot of courage for Lane. "What would you think about painting this emblem on my barn?"

She looked up at him and playfully batted her eyelashes.

"Now, Mr. Curry, don't be fooling around with a girl's affections," she teased.

The playfulness caught Lane off guard. He was scrambling to come up with an appropriately light response when she saved him.

"I love big projects. I feel so constrained sometimes trying to scale everything so it will fit in someone's bedroom. How big is the barn?"

"It's about twenty feet high and about sixty feet long."

"Yes, I'll do it," Mary almost gushed. "I need to come look at it and take exact measurements. Can I keep this?" She held up the can.

She showed up at the house right after lunch. Lane and Steve took her to the barn and helped her measure. For the first time, Lane realized that drivers would be able to see the painting as soon as they rounded the curve where the highway crossed the Cucharas River heading up the mountain. It would be quite an unexpected eyeful. Mary rolled up her tape measure and finished her freestyle sketch of the barn with the dimensions in the margins.

"I understand the original house is over one hundred years old?" she asked as she walked toward her Jeep. "You know the whole village was just atwitter when you started to remodel. Everyone had a rumor about what you were doing with the old place."

"No, I didn't." Laughed Lane. "Would you like to see it and become the village expert?"

"Yes, I would. I love old things."

"We tore down a wall right here so the living area would be more open and so the wood stove would better heat the downstairs. The wood stove is new, of course. The old ones just don't heat as efficiently. These interior walls used to be green, but we wanted more light, so we painted them all white. These walls here are part of the original cabin. They're rock and mortar covered with stucco. These wood floors are original, but we did have to refinish them."

"You did a great job with them," Mary said.

"The built-in kitchen cabinets were added about thirty years ago, and we had to build new counter tops and add a new sink, and of course, the bathrooms are all new. Watch your step. Steve's room is down here. These are the original beams. This room was probably used to house some domestic livestock. We added the bathroom and the smaller wood stove."

Showing the house and retelling its history reminded Lane how proud of it he was. They moved back upstairs.

Mary was visibly impressed. She said, "You've done a wonderful job. It's even more wonderful that you have such an attachment to it."

Lane told her the story about the Bright and Early coffee can and his last camping trip with his grandfather.

She didn't say anything but looked at him for a minute.

"I'll make you proud of the barn, I promise."

She turned to go and noticed a group of family photos on the shelves by the front door. "Steve, your mom was beautiful."

Steve was at a loss for words. Even though he and Lane were much more open about his mom, he was not used to talking to strangers about her.

"What was she like?" Mary was looking right at Steve. Lane instinctively wanted to protect Steve. They had both worked so hard lately to be more open and to talk about Becky and her death. And now, Mary was about to spoil all of it by pushing Steve.

Steve looked back at Mary. No one had asked him that question before. Mary's words and her voice and her bright eyes bore right through his sadness and any anger.

"She had a great sense of humor even when she fussed at me. She used to make me laugh a lot. She could always make me feel better whenever I had a problem. She could get me to talk, you know? When I didn't want to, she made me want to. I knew that she was always on my side no matter what, and that made me feel really—I don't know—safe, I guess."

Lane didn't say a word. He was transfixed. Mary only offered the occasional nod or maybe "I know what you mean." Steve rambled on telling Mary about his mom and their times together and even some of his struggles after her death. He told her about the search and rescue in the mountains and how getting to know the general had affected him.

Then he seemed to run out of emotional gas and stopped talking.

Mary put her hand on Steve's arm and said, "I think you were very lucky to have such a wonderful mom, and I know it was a terrible loss for you and your dad. I feel very honored that you felt like you could share your feelings with me." She turned and looked at Lane, who was battling a host of emotions. He walked her out to her Jeep.

"I don't quite know what to say," he told her.

"Let's concentrate on your barn for now," she said and drove off.

And concentrate she did. She had Lane and Steve apply two coats of base paint to the side of the barn. The old, dry wooden planks thirstily sucked up the first two coats of paint Lane sprayed on. They used rollers with long extension handles to apply two more coats. By the end of the first week, the side of the barn was ready for art.

Mary arrived soon after daylight the next day and climbed up on the makeshift scaffolding Lane and Steve had erected. It wasn't very pretty, but it was safe, and it allowed Mary to walk from one end of her giant canvas to the other. She began with chalk and drew the image and the letters on the side of the barn. Then she stood back a good thirty to fifty feet and looked at her work in progress. She took several digital photos, which she later downloaded to her PC and enlarged to help her judge whether or not the scale was correct.

The next morning, Lane heard the Jeep as Mary pulled into the driveway and parked. He poured two cups of hot coffee and headed out the front door. Mary was opening the first of several buckets of paint—red, yellow, and white.

"I thought this might help you get started." Lane handed her the coffee cup.

"Oh, thanks. We're making good progress, don't you think?" she asked.

"It looks terrific," Lane said. "How on earth do you figure out the proper measurements to use?"

"I can't explain it. I just see a picture in my mind and I keep comparing that mental image to what I'm putting on the canvas. It's not that much different from what I do on a normal canvas, it's just bigger."

She caused quite a commotion on Highway 12 once she got the first colors on the gray, dull barn. Traffic that normally sped by at fifty miles per hour slowed drastically as drivers craned to look at the outdoor art in progress. Several pulled off to the side to take pictures.

She worked fast, rarely needing to paint over mistakes. Using long strokes, she covered a lot of area quickly, returning with smaller brushes to fill in details. It was exhausting work, and by the time the light began to fade, Mary was beat.

Lane and Steve met her at the Jeep.

"Why don't you let us treat you to dinner at the Timbers to celebrate your first day's progress."

"That's the best idea I've heard all day. Let me clean up and I'll meet you there."

The Curry Home

Lane thought he noticed a sparkle in her eyes but quickly dismissed the idea.

The mural was finished by the end of the second week and had become the talk of the valley. The *Valley View* ran a story with a photo. The traffic past the Curry place had picked up considerably but soon waned once all the local residents had driven by to "ooh and ah." The dinner threesome of Lane, Steve, and Mary soon became a fixture at the Timbers. The Currys learned that Mary Kingsley had grown up in Durango, Colorado, attended the local Fort Lewis College (the campus in the sky) and had graduated with an art degree, which was really just a postscript to her "real" art education, lovingly rendered by her grandmother, who had put a brush in her hand at age three. She moved to

Cuchara while desperately fleeing a truly horrendous marriage that had ended even worse. As she guardedly spoke about her failed marriage, Lane, for the first time since he had met her, noticed a shadow overtake her mood and subdue her usual bright expression. Later, putting together graduation dates and doing some quick mental math, Lane decided that she was around thirty-five years old. He wondered what had happened to her ex-husband, but he did not feel like intruding. Joe filled in other details and facts; she was absolutely broke when she arrived in Cuchara. Joe had put her to work waiting tables at the Timbers, and she had traded some art work for meals. Joe hung several of her paintings on the restaurant's walls and refused to take a commission when they started selling. Soon, Mary no longer needed to wait tables as she achieved some financial success with her paintings. But whenever Joe was short of waitress, Mary would fill in without accepting pay or tips. She waited tables with grace and poise, her quick and pleasant smile pulling the diners into easy conversation. Yet she could muster lightning-quick verbal barbs for the occasional you're-never-going-to-please-me boorish tourist or the falling-down-drunk golfer.

Lane had grown used to mourning. It didn't make sense that Mary made him feel like a giddy high school kid. How could he be attracted to another woman after losing Becky just—what was it?—almost three years ago? His and Becky's college courtship was traditional, expected, and predictable. But this was more like a lightning bolt. Lane caught himself thinking about Mary at random moments during his day. He found excuses to go to the Timbers and sit in one of Joe's aspen rocking chairs, hoping Mary would wander out of her studio. He found Mary irresistible, but he was wracked with guilt for having those feelings. Was there any chance Mary shared some of these feelings or would she laugh or be appalled if he shared them? Of course, the minute he thought he might have rationalized a coherent plan to explore them with her, he would agonize about Steve. How could he possibly tell Steve that he was—what—thinking about dating again? How did a man his age date anyway? It would probably be laughable. So he fought his emotional battle alone, scared to death of appearing foolish and scaring her off, appalled at the thought of insulting Becky's memory. Maybe he was just infatuated with Mary and he should forget about making any romantic confessions to her and be satisfied with having found a new friend.

DOUBLE BLACK DIAMONDS

Steve zipped his new Columbia ski jacket and nervously pulled at his gloves. He and Chris were about to ride Lift Three to the top of the ski mountain. The resort was not open yet, and a handful of employees were preparing for the upcoming Colorado Tramway Board lift inspection. As the director of the ski patrol, Chris would ski down all the ski runs before opening to the public to assure there were no dangerous obstacles for skiers. He would also position the equipment at the four ski patrol huts, which were located atop each of the resort's four ski lifts. Steve, as a member of the junior ski patrol, was along to help and to learn about his new responsibilities. They pushed into the lanes and lined up for the chair lift. Steve shifted his poles to his outside hand and looked over his inside shoulder, anticipating the chair. The edge of the moving chair hit the back of his knees; he sat down, and they were airborne, their skis dangling below the chair as they accelerated toward the top of Lift Three.

The season's first real snowstorm had dumped almost three feet of fresh powder on Cuchara, and resort management was scrambling to get the ski mountain groomed to establish a solid snow base for the upcoming ski season. The resort needed at least thirty inches of base snow for decent skiing. The earlier the base was packed down, the better chance that subsequent snow would stick and not melt as quickly. The more snow they could build up now, the better the ski conditions would be for opening day. Artificial snowmaking machines roared as they spewed thousands of gallons of water into the freezing air where it was transformed into snow to enhance the fresh natural snow.

Steve had taken to skiing the first time he awkwardly slid down the mountain with Chris (who skied backward with his skis in an exaggerated V) in front of him and who instructed him, "Keep your weight over your skis, knees bent, shins pressing the inside of your boots; don't look at your skis; look out front—at me. Shift your weight slightly from left to right to left to turn." By the end of the first day, Steve was skiing with his skis parallel and executing turns whenever he wanted. The outdoors inspired him, and the views from the top of Grandote, the resort's longest and widest ski run, were breathtaking. West Peak dominated the landscape with the rich greens of fir trees in stark contrast to the brilliant white of the snow fields. The fluid grace of skiing, the physical challenge to maintain control at high speeds, constantly monitoring the feel of the snow and the changing topography of the slope, and the seamless coordination of the senses and the body exhilarated Steve. He could never ski too fast. He was fearless regardless of the steepness of the slope or the conditions of the snow. Chris had taught him to adjust his stance and "ski mentality" when skiing in deep powder. Moguls, those knee-pounding bumps on the slopes, required a different rhythm with obsessive focus and reflexive knee action. By the end of his first season at Cuchara, Steve could ski expertly in all conditions and on all terrain. He could transition between groomed, smooth snow to the un-groomed deep powder of the custom-made trails that whipsawed through the trees and between the regular slopes, to spine-jarring moguls—the steeper the better. Skiing was not his dad's sport. There was no history of family ski prowess, no basis for comparison or disappointment. Steve became the family expert.

As a member of the junior ski patrol, Steve would assist the ski patrol members with patrolling the slopes to deter out-of-control skiers, providing assistance and directions to skiers unfamiliar with the mountain, and assisting injured skiers. Skiers who could not get themselves down to the first-aid clinic were transported in long red sleds, in which they either lay (heads downhill) or sat upright. A ski patrol member would ski the sled down the mountain. Steve would learn how to ski with a sled in case of emergency, such as mass casualties, but would not routinely treat or transport injured skiers.

While Steve was enjoying his status as the first skier of the year at Cuchara Valley Ski Resort, Lane was listening to Will Poteet, the general manager of the resort, about the problems of operating the resort for absentee owners. Lane knew more about and was more involved with the ski resort than he wanted to be. As pre-opening activity had picked up, Lane had offered to give up his tiny office space in the resort's building, but Will had gotten used to sounding off to Lane and had even begun asking his advice.

The resort was built in the early eighties by a group of wealthy Texas businessmen in concert with local ranchers. They had borrowed close to $30 million from a Texas savings and loan company. After a couple of years of marginal operations, the resort was desperately short of cash. Unfortunately, the savings and loan industry was suffering from a plethora of their own self-inflicted wounds, and the resort's lender cut off all funding to the resort, forcing the owners into foreclosure. The resort was now operating under its fourth set of owners. Will had been there from the beginning, first as the resort's mountain manager, then as the resort's supposed undertaker as the Resolution Trust Corporation (the federal government's hastily legislated bail-out vehicle) swallowed many failing savings and loan companies, including the one that had foreclosed on the Cuchara Valley Ski Resort. Many valley residents considered the resort beyond saving as soon as it disappeared into the maw of a federal government agency. Looking back over the tattered history of the resort, Lane wondered if it wouldn't have been more humane to let the resort die a natural death. It had always faced a variety of daunting challenges—geographically, topographically, and meteorologically. It was too far south. The weather was unpredictable. If it wasn't an unseasonably warm day in January, it was the fierce Chinook winds stripping the meager snow from the slopes. Sometimes the snow just wouldn't show up for days or weeks at a time, requiring the snowmaking machines to run overtime, depleting the water level in Baker Creek as well as the resort's cash balances. With marginal snowfall, the resort often had to offer discount ski trips to groups who were miserly spenders when they did show up. The historical financial records Lane had seen reflected a steadily deteriorating financial condition as the fixed overhead costs devoured cash faster than any marketing plan could replace.

The current owner, another wealthy Texas businessman, was questioning Will's budget for the coming year.

"He prepared his own budget based on what the last owners told him and won't listen to me or look at past financial records," Will lamented to Lane. "I've told him over and over that we need to replace over one hundred thousand dollars of snow-grooming equipment, and if we expect to keep Lift Five open all season, we have to extend the snowmaking to at least here."

Will pointed out the ski runs on the wall-mounted trail map as if he expected Lane to approve the budget. Lane was a good listener and offered his advice when he thought appropriate. It was beyond comprehension why the most recent owner had plopped down almost $4 million to buy a distressed ski resort without having someone audit the financial statements first and at least prepare a projected cash-flow statement. The numbers Lane had seen clearly showed the resort could not break-even with less than about thirty-five skiers. Last year, only twenty-two thousand skiers, many of those with discounted lift tickets, had skied at Cuchara. Lane's own meager research on the ski industry revealed that all but two or three of the largest, most successful ski resorts lost money on their ski operations. They made it up by selling very high-priced real estate—houses and condos, for example—and by charging exorbitant rentals for base-area retail space. Not only that, the ski industry nationwide was virtually flat, with competition among the established ski resorts growing fiercer by the year. A small ski resort without an overwhelming competitive advantage had little hope of surviving, much less prospering. On average, about 11.5 million skiers visited Colorado each year, and the ski industry was dominated by Vail, Aspen, Breckenridge, Winter Park, and Beaver Creek. Cuchara billed itself as a family resort but lacked enough rentable rooms in the valley to be considered a true destination resort. Cuchara advertised heavily in the Colorado markets but lacked the really challenging black-diamond expert slopes that Western slope resorts, like those close to Denver, offered. Wolf Creek and Monarch were both within commuting distance from Cuchara and siphoned off many potential customers.

If an entire community could be bipolar, that would describe Cuchara's relationship with the ski resort. As opening day approached and the resort increased hiring, the hopes of the local business community (which prospered and suffered as the fortunes of the resort ebbed and flowed) soared. When the snow was scarce and the resort had to lay off employees, the mood soured and rumors raced through the community like wildfire, feeding off their fears and dashed hopes.

Lane left Will's office and wandered outside, looking up the slopes to catch a glimpse of Steve. He trudged up through the snow toward the warming hut for a closer look. There was activity on the large wooden deck, so he walked around to the entrance, picking his way through a stack of boxes. The front door was propped open, and a couple of young men were ferrying boxes inside. Lane picked up a couple of them and carried them indoors.

"Hey, Professor, watch it or I'll put you to serious work." Mary appeared from the back, clad in her trademark overalls. "Okay, guys. Thanks a lot for the help." She shook hands with the two high school helpers as they exited the front door and closed it behind them.

"I almost didn't recognize you without an easel and brush," Lane teased, pleased about the surprise meeting.

"Well, get used to it. Joe hired me to operate the warming hut for the ski season. The resort was desperate to have him and Ernie take charge of it, and since they expect a busy season at the Timbers, they asked me to oversee operations. I've worked so closely with them at the Timbers that I know the routine. And this will be a fairly simple operation since the menu is so basic. The tough part will be keeping enough employees interested for such low wages. We'll have to rely on high school kids mostly, and they make for a very unpredictable work force," Mary said.

"That will play havoc with your painting though, won't it?" Lane asked.

"Sure, but as declared in some famous movie, 'reality bites.' Joe made me a really good offer and I can use the money. Here, have a cup of coffee on me." Mary handed him a cup, and they sat down, alone in the empty, disheveled dining area.

Mary continued, "I saw Steve ride up the lift with Chris. This place must be heaven for a kid like him."

"I can't imagine a better place for Steve at this stage of his life," Lane said. "I had some serious reservations about my decision to move here during our first year. It occurred to me that maybe I was just running away from Becky's death."

Mary hesitated a moment. They had never ventured here before, and she wasn't sure how or even if she should go there now. "I know how devastating a broken marriage can be, but I can't imagine what it would be like to lose a spouse and then to deal with a child." Mary had jumped in with both feet.

"Steve and I are both doing a lot better."

Lane's heart skipped a beat. This was the opening he had been waiting for.

"At first I never imagined that I could ever feel anything but grief. Now I know that time softens the grief and that affection can heal heartache. I'm feeling that affection right now, Mary. You came into my life, totally unexpected, and swept the ache from my heart."

Lane blinked and looked at Mary. She was leaning forward, expectantly watching his face. Lane realized he had just delivered his self-practiced soliloquy to himself. His speech center had completely shut down! His brain had turned to mush. He was beginning to sweat. If he had not turned away so abruptly, he would have seen the anticipation in Mary's expression.

"Listen, I know you've got a lot of work to do. I should get out of your way." Lane hurried away, sure his pounding heart would betray him.

Mary slumped back in her chair. Her mind was screaming at Lane, "Tell me! Tell me! I want to hear." She knew he had been struggling with his feelings. She had noticed several clues: his eyes seemed to soften as they caressed her face, and if she turned abruptly, she could catch him watching her with a tender look in his eyes.

Irony of ironies, she thought. *For the last ten years, I've built my own emotional wall of self defense, able to withstand the most determined emotional assault. Maybe my great wall of denial has become permanent and is more visible to others than I thought. Would I even be able to return his feelings?* She didn't have an answer.

Lane pulled off Highway 12 into the village of Cuchara. After leaving Mary at the warming hut, he decided he needed a distraction, and the Dog Bar was always good for that. It was too early in the season for skiers, so the Dog Bar's late-afternoon patrons were mostly locals, including some of the resort's early hires who were done for the day. Princess greeted him when he sat down. She was the owners' gentile St. Bernard who unofficially ruled Cuchara Avenue and had appeared in hundreds of tourist photos over the years. She received the obligatory pat on the head from Lane and wandered off, never one to overstay her welcome.

"Hello, Professor." Jerry Anderson sat down at Lane's table. Lane winced at the sound of the overworn greeting. He was trying his best to like it, but it still sounded too new to his ears. And he secretly wondered if it wasn't meant as a minor insult to his position in academics. Probably not. Mary had started it, and he knew her too well to consider it anything but a respectful and good-natured acknowledgement of his teaching position.

AN ENTICING OFFER

Jerry was the most seasoned realtor in either LaVeta or Cuchara and the one who had helped Lane negotiate his earlier rental agreement. His real expertise was ranch property on both sides of Highway 12 between LaVeta and Trinidad. He virtually owned the listing and selling rights along the entire Highway of Legends due to his credentials as a lifelong resident and his friendships with every major land owner. His father had been a rancher as had his grandfather. Jerry knew the family histories and many of the family secrets that haunted Highway 12. Lane especially liked the rural legend of the unnamed rancher who, while excavating for a new ranch house, came upon an intact human skeleton. Knowing how quickly it would attract archeologists and law enforcement and who knew who else, he ceremoniously leaned the remains against the earth wall and proceeded to build his house on top of it. He figured that was every bit as much respect as a bunch of university types and small-town deputy sheriffs would afford it anyway. Lane liked Jerry. He had a quick mind and encyclopedic knowledge of all facets of Colorado rural real estate, and Lane knew he could be trusted.

"Hi, Jerry. Can I buy you a beer?" Lane pulled a chair from the table for Jerry to take.

"Thanks." He shook Lane's hand and sat down. He was as comfortable drinking beer with a university professor as with a local rancher who had never traveled further than Pueblo.

They talked for a few minutes about the resort and its prospects for the coming ski season and about the number of hunters in the valley for elk and deer season.

"I got an interesting call from a real estate broker in Denver," Jerry offered as he emptied his beer mug. "I've done a lot of business with this guy, and he's always on the lookout for attractive property in this area, but he expressed specific interest in your place. He seemed to know you had restored the house and had leased your grass during the summer. He asked me a few real estate-type questions, but it was obvious he already knew a lot about your property. Then he almost too casually asked me if you were interested in selling. I know you're not but wanted you to know that someone asked the question." Jerry paid for a fresh round.

"You're right about not being even remotely interested in selling, but thanks. Any ideas on why this guy zeroed in on my land?"

"I didn't at first. This was almost two weeks ago, but it took me a while to remember something that came up a couple of years ago when I was helping a water attorney do some title searches in this area. He was working for a large consortium that had purchased several thousand acres of land in the San Luis Valley for the purpose of selling the accompanying water rights to another out-of-state group who wanted to build a pipeline to Denver and sell water to the city. Their efforts were eventually crushed in court, but we all know there's big money out there looking to move water to Denver and other front-range cities to support the urban sprawl." Jerry paused for a minute. "Anyway, back to your property. I did some research and put together a list of the water rights owned by the major land owners in the valley and discovered your family was among the first land owners to acquire water rights in the valley. That means all the water rights that are attached to your property are number one rights. Essentially, your water rights come ahead of anyone who owns number two, number three rights, or later." Jerry leaned forward. "Number one water rights are naturally more valuable. Because your property has not changed hands, water rights have never come up and you probably didn't even know you owned them. Along with your one hundred fifty acres of land, you own about two hundred water rights."

Lane listened with interest, but since he would never sell the property, he simply filed the information away.

"Well, I gotta go and baby sit a looker from Texas. Good to see you." Jerry slapped Lane's shoulder as he left. By now, the Dog Bar was full and getting louder by the minute. Lane could faintly hear music, real music, not jukebox noise. He could see a group around the piano, and he stood up to move closer. A tall, heavyset man was sitting at the piano, warming up the keys. A scruffy local, who Lane recognized, was tuning a guitar, and a young teenager was blending in with a harmonica. Lane saw Joe and Ernie enter and watched them until they caught his eye. They joined him at his table. By now, the ad hoc musical trio had launched into a rousing musical mix that had the whole crowd clapping and singing along.

"Who are those guys?" Lane laughed.

Joe told him, "The piano player is Reggie's dad. He's a professional musician and has played all over the country with some of the biggest jazz bands. Since he retired to Corpus Christi a few years back, he spends a few weeks each year around here visiting and annoying Reggie and playing with local musicians whenever the mood strikes. He can play anything with anybody. He always puts out a tip jar and gives it all to his pick-up accompanists. He's a real character and a real good guy."

Ernie was laughing. "Two years ago, he was visiting when Reggie was trying to get her hay put up. She always cuts and bales her own hay and sells what she doesn't need for her own horses. She had it all cut and baled and needed to pick it up off the ground so she could deliver some to her customers and store the rest in her barn. Her truck had broken down and wouldn't be fixed for two or three days. She was beside herself, so her dad drove his 1989 Cadillac down to the Rancho Not So Grande, hooked up her hay trailer to it, and Reggie and her hired hands loaded every single bale of hay. There were nonstop cars and trucks driving past her place as the word spread. By the time they were done, the rear end of his caddie was practically dragging the ground, but he never blinked an eye. He wouldn't help unload the hay, but he sure knew how to get a job done." Ernie was laughing so hard he almost couldn't finish the story.

Lane better understood Reggie's stubborn streak now. It was genetic. Reggie must have gotten her good nature from her dad too. He was clearly enjoying himself with the rowdy crowd in the Dog Bar.

One evening several weeks later, by which time Lane had forgotten about his conversation with Jerry, his phone rang.

"Mr. Curry?"

"Yes."

"My name is Bret Sadler. I'm a real estate broker in Denver, and I represent a client who would like to make you a generous offer for your property in Cuchara. He's offering you three thousand five hundred dollars an acre. I would like to—"

Lane interrupted, "Does your client understand there are substantial water rights associated with this property?"

After only a slight hesitation, the broker continued.

"He assumed his above-market offer would include all water rights."

No, Lane thought, *he assumed that, like most Texans, I don't have a clue about water rights.*

Lane shot back, "Send me an offer letter with an itemized offer for the land and the water rights and I'll consider it." Lane had no intention of considering it, but he was curious and was willing to play along for a bit. "Is there anything else?"

"Uh, no. We'll get back to you."

Lane decided it was time to get smart about water rights since someone obviously wanted his. He started by visiting John Reynolds, the district manager of the Cuchara Sanitation and Water District. John briefly explained how water rights were valued and sold in the district.

"Our water rights are designated as EQRs or Equivalent Quantity Ratios. One EQR equates to an acre foot, which is the volume of water required to cover one acre of land to a depth of one foot, three hundred twenty-five thousand eight hundred fifty gallons to be exact, which is the theoretical amount of water it takes to supply a family of four for one year."

He went on to explain that water rights were sold separately from land and were viewed by the courts in Colorado as "property rights." He went on to explain that single-family homes had to purchase one EQR from the district before they could be connected to the district water system. The price of a water tap, the mechanism by which water rights were sold to property owners for domestic use, was currently five thousand dollars. This was, in effect, a way to charge homeowners a fee to help pay for developing and maintaining enough water rights to service the district. Colorado had the highest cost of water in the nation. Broomfield, Colorado, charged new homeowners over twenty thousand dollars to connect water service. Assuming someone bought your water rights for the purpose of moving them, they would be worth in the neighborhood of twenty thousand dollars per EQR. Lane did some mental arithmetic and couldn't believe his water rights might be worth as much as $40 million dollars. He rejected the number as outlandish.

EQRs can be bought and sold on the open market. For example, ranchers had sold some of their water rights to the ski resort when it was first developed. The resort needed large amounts of water rights for their condos and for snowmaking. So even though Baker Creek flowed through the resort property, the resort could not divert any of it to use unless they owned the appropriate number of water rights. Lane remembered hearing a discussion in the resort office about the dilemma the resort faced by storing the water diverted from Baker Creek in the small one-acre pond near the maintenance garage. This pond was used to accumulate the diverted water that was used for snowmaking. The only problem—the resort owned only direct-use water rights, not storage rights. So they were technically in violation of their usage permits by storing this water.

"There are lots of farmers in eastern Colorado who are being offered large sums of money for their agricultural water rights. Large water developers want to move this water to use in Colorado Springs and Denver to accommodate the growth in population. Naturally, there is a huge controversy because once these farmers give up their water rights, they have no way to continue farming or ranching, and many small communities will dry up and blow away," John explained. "You probably heard about the attempt to hijack hundreds of thousands of acre-feet of ground water from the San Luis Valley and move it to Denver. Developers are willing to spend hundreds of millions of dollars to grab water rights wherever they can because Denver and Colorado Springs and other front-range cities will pay billions of dollars, which they can collect from residents, over future years to get more water. Approximately eighty-eight percent of Colorado's population lives in the South Platte and Arkansas basins, whose rivers carry only fifteen percent of the state's natural stream flows. So the only way the cities can fuel their growth is by buying and moving water. To complicate matters even more, Colorado is bound by certain interstate decrees to leave certain volumes of water in its rivers for the use of other states downstream.

Once they own the water rights, a buyer still has to get through Colorado Water Court to use it elsewhere, but those who oppose selling rural water rights out from under their communities don't want the issue to get that far. With the state's growth and economic well-being at stake, who knows which way the courts or the state legislature will bend?"

Lane took it all in and said, "You're saying that if I sold my water rights, they could conceivably be moved to Denver to water a golf course?"

John smiled. "That's it in a nutshell."

Lane just had another unsettling thought. "How else might a water developer go after water rights if the owner refused to sell?"

"There are a couple of legal attacks on a water owner's right to their water. One is to claim that the rights have been abandoned if the rights have not been used for an extended period. If someone other than the water's decreed owner was somehow able to use it for a continuous period of eighteen years, the new user could claim adverse use and they might be entitled to claim legal ownership."

Lane asked a couple more technical questions and left better informed but apprehensive. He was wondering if the act of leasing his grass for cattle grazing would qualify as beneficial use of the property's water rights and cushion him against a claim of abandonment of those rights.

The ski season was off to a shaky start. The resort had opened with marginal snow in the middle of December and ran the snowmaking every night to try and salvage the skied-down slopes. The groomers, large tractorlike vehicles with blades (much like a snow plow) roared up and down the slopes all night to smooth out the snow, and to move snow from under the trees to cover bare spots on the ski runs. From a distance, they looked like giant fireflies suspended in the frozen mountain. It took a small army of employees to run the snowmaking, operate the giant groomers, and perform maintenance on the lifts. That was one reason the resort's overhead costs were so extremely high. The resort had to spend a certain amount of money on maintaining its equipment and the slopes, regardless of how many skiers bought tickets.

Lane spent several days of the month at his office on campus and occasionally traveled to Denver to conduct seminars. Most other days found him in his resort office taking care of various classroom chores like grading papers or working on his newest idea for a book. He had regained his intellectual fervor. Fridays he would spend on the slopes to ski with (behind) Steve. He would also try to visit with Mary at the warming hut, but Fridays and weekends usually proved to be fairly busy and offered little chance to spend time with her. The Timbers seemed to be chronically short on weekends, so Mary would close up the warming hut and rush to the Timbers to help them out. She was in a perpetual state of exhaustion and didn't have much time to think about Lane. She knew she missed being around him and wondered if maybe they were destined to just drift slowly along on their separate journeys of loneliness.

THE PERFECT STORM

In late December, the jet stream took an unseasonable dip into the southern states and opened up the frigid freeway from Canada. A Canadian clipper roared into Colorado, plunging temperatures to new lows. Cuchara's temperatures plummeted to minus twenty degrees in a matter of hours. The wind roared down the mountain, dropping the wind chill to minus forty degrees. A low-pressure area was squatting over Albuquerque and sucked prodigious amounts of moisture from the Gulf of Mexico and funneled it right to Cuchara. The snow began falling at rates exceeding one inch per hour and was whipped around in dizzying circles by the screaming winds. Snowplows battled to keep Highway 12 passable, but the drifting snow would cover the road as quickly as the giant blades could clear it. Visibility was no better than a few feet. The entire world went white. The wind felt like a million needles on exposed skin.

Highway 12 with winter coat

Lane kept waiting for the wind to lighten up before heading for home. He was at the Timbers when it started, and he sat in the lobby with one of Joe's hot toddies waiting for a chance to visit with Mary. Most of the customers had left, hurrying home before the storm got any worse. Joe told Mary she needed to go home. He and Ernie lived in the apartment above the restaurant and could easily finish cleaning up.

"You don't want to try to walk home in this," Lane stood up. "Let me drive you. The snow is already knee deep, and you're liable to get frost bite."

Mary was too tired to object. She just wanted to get off her feet and was glad for someone to take charge for the time being. She had to make decisions all day long and keep her high school student employees motivated. They seemed to remember only what she had told them ten minutes ago.

Even with four-wheel drive engaged, the Suburban struggled against the thickening snow. The extreme temperature froze the snow onto the wiper blades as they rhythmically clunked back and forth. Lane pulled into Mary's narrow driveway. He left the engine running, and the heater turned up full blast. He zipped up his ski jacket and pulled on his stocking cap. Mary held on to his arm as he plowed through the knee-deep snow to her front door. Fortunately, her cabin was small and she had lit a fire in her wood stove before leaving.

They hurried through the door and closed it behind them as the wind blasted through the brief opening.

"Oh, thanks. I've never seen such a violent storm," Mary gasped as she shook the snow out of her hair. She undid her heavy coat and slid it off. Lane hung it up for her. It seemed awfully warm to him as he looked at Mary's face, barely six inches from his own. Her eyes were bright and her face was flushed—from the wind, he guessed. Her hair flowed down her neck onto her shoulders. A few spots of melted snow sparkled in the dim light. He could hear the fresh aspen logs crackling in the fire as the wind howled and battered the small cabin.

"You know, there's something I want to tell you," Lane almost whispered as he reached out and gently took her arm.

"I know. I know," Mary said so softly that Lane couldn't hear the words, but he could read her lips as they moved closer.

He took her in his arms and buried his face in her hair.

"Oh, God. What took you so long?" she whispered.

His mouth found hers. Again. And again.

The wind exhausted itself the second day of the storm, but the snow continued for another two days. Forty-four inches of fresh snow smothered the valley by the time the storm had ended. The temperature sluggishly inched upward into the teens as the sun returned with a flourish. Lane had never seen anything so beautiful. The deep snow seemed to muffle even the slightest sound. The giant ponderosa pines were even more majestic wearing their soft white crowns outlined against the splendor of the clear, blue sky.

Chris had cleared the Curry's driveway. The resulting snow piles on either side made for a dreamlike journey through a white canyon to get out to the highway. Even though the temperature never reached above the twenties for several days, the sun would not be denied. Its warming rays cut through the frigid air and began melting away the near-record snowfall.

LaVeta had closed school for two days, and the resort had shut down as well. Steve and Lane were both suffering from severe cabin fever. Steve was shoveling snow from the porch while Sampson frolicked in the powdered yard. Lane needed to get out also. He pulled on his coat and struggled with his dilemma. No question about it. He was smitten with Mary; transformed, overwhelmed, and transfixed also came to mind. His conscience tried to whisper a muffled objection in tribute to Becky's memory, but Lane gently overruled it. He turned all of his attention to the question of how to tell Steve. How was he going to react if Steve resisted the idea? Or was appalled at the thought of Lane sullying the memory of his mom? What if Lane had to choose between driving Steve away and continuing a relationship with Mary? He still didn't know what lay ahead for Mary and him.

Steve came in the house after brushing loose snow from his stocking cap and pulled off his gloves. He was laughing.

"Do you see Sampson? He's going crazy in the snow."

Lane peered out the front window. Sampson was barreling through a snow bank that was twice as tall as he was, snow flying in all directions. He emerged covered with snow, and icy whiskers drooped from his muzzle.

Lane decided he needed to tell Steve now. His heart raced as he steeled himself for the look on Steve's face.

"Steve, you and Mary get along pretty well, don't you?"

"Sure. I like her a lot. Why?"

The lengthy, labored explanation of how his feelings for Becky would never diminish and how he would never do anything to tarnish her memory and how he really wanted Steve to understand the changing nature of Lane's feelings flew right out the window.

"Well, I've decided to ask Mary out for a date."

He studied Steve's face for a sign. Any sign. The corner of Steve's mouth twitched before he spoke.

"Gee, Dad, what took you so long? I mean she's been hot for you for a long time." Steve grinned.

It turned out Steve and Mary had actually discussed Lane and his reluctance to declare his feelings for quite some time. He and Mary had become quite close, as Steve had gravitated to her warmth and sincerity. It was Steve who first broached the subject of Mary and Lane. Mary had told him that, yes, she was attracted to his dad and enjoyed his company. She had confided in Steve about her own failed marriage and how she had vowed never to marry again. Her frankness and her trust in Steve, speaking to him like one adult to another, opened the door for Steve to trust her in return. He was already sold on Mary. He just wasn't as giddy as his dad was.

The storm had increased the ski resort's base to seventy-five inches and raised spirits up and down the valley. The snowmaking machines went silent, and the groomers worked diligently to pack down the fresh snow on Grandote, the primary intermediate ski run. Most skiers, especially beginners, could not handle the fresh powder. Will had decided to leave Diablo, their only expert ski run, un-groomed, as only seasoned skiers would be on it. The fresh powder would provide a daunting ski experience on the narrow, steep slope. One of the resort's weaknesses was the lack of expert ski runs, and Will wanted to exploit Diablo's difficulty every chance he got.

The monumental snowfall and a shot of fresh advertising along the front range boosted the resort's attendance. A number of cabin owners from Oklahoma and Texas descended on Cuchara soon after the storm and helped fuel the financial respite. Equipment breakdowns, rising costs such as workmen's compensation insurance, and utilities continued to threaten its economic survival though.

Steve was exhausted, as usual, after skiing all day. He had skied with the ski patrol and had helped numerous skiers extricate themselves from the deep powder. It lured the younger, less-experienced skiers into the trees, away from the established trails. Not used to the deep powder, they inevitably fell and lost their skis. Usually, they were not injured, so the junior ski patrol would help them locate their skis, get them back to the trail, and give them the spiel about not skiing between trees.

A BRUSH WITH THE PAST

He began to unlayer his ski clothing while the freshly lit fire in the wood stove began to gain momentum. Once it caught, it would heat his semi-basement room quickly. Steve had laid claim to his room the moment he laid eyes on it. The old farmhouse was built on a slope, and the bottom floor was surrounded on two sides by earth. The back wall had a door that opened onto the back of their property. The walls were solid rock, and the floor was hard wood. Steve had his own wood stove, and after it burned all night, the walls would radiate heat most of the next day. He liked the room because it was open and spacious, plus it afforded him a little bit of cherished privacy. They had added a small bathroom when they remodeled, so he and his dad did not have to compete for the shower. His bed was in the middle of the space, the bathroom at one end and the stove in the corner next to the bathroom. The opposite end of the room served as his study corner and contained the only piece of furniture they had been able to salvage from the old house. It was Steve who had found the old desk in a corner of the big barn. With help from the shop teacher at school, Steve had restored it into a useful, if not aesthetically pleasing, desk. Steve had also discovered a small wooden box full of documents and letters, folded and aged. He had put the box and its discolored documents in the bottom drawer of the refurbished desk and had promptly forgotten about them.

That night, after drying off from his shower and enjoying the warmth of the now roaring fire, he sat down in the desk chair. He had been thinking about enrolling in the EMT course, which would be offered during the coming summer, and was going to read over the application if he could just find it. He opened all the desk drawers, rummaged through their contents, and saw the forgotten box of old documents in the back of the bottom drawer. He sat them on top of the desk, intending to give them to his dad later.

It was a couple of weeks before Lane remembered the worn-out pages that Steve had given him. The end of the fall semester had caught him by surprise, and he became very busy in the frantic, waning days. Finally, he had submitted student grades and wrapped up the last lingering administrative chores. He reveled in the freedom of the break that lay ahead.

He unfolded the aged pages gingerly. He supposed the very low humidity had helped preserve the documents. Beneath the folded pages lay the remnants of a newspaper article that had not weathered time's journey as well as the heavier papers. The headline was barely legible. "Local Man Presumed Dead" was what Lane could make out. Reading the article was like listening to someone who stuttered.

> *... missing ... six months ... body ... mysterious ... Chaparral ... respected member ... rancher ... survived by wife ... Sweden ... foul play not ... led out*

Reading the broken prose several times over allowed Lane to discern the skeleton of the article's content. A local rancher had been missing for six months; his last known whereabouts was in the vicinity of Chaparral Falls. The sheriff had not ruled out foul play but did not have any evidence either way. Lane wondered if Sven Curry was the missing rancher. He had never known the circumstances of Sven's death. In fact, he knew very little about his father's family. For that matter, he knew very little about his father. He set the tattered article aside and unfolded a letter to Sven Curry.

Dear Mr. Curry,

I am pleased to present to you the assay report on the sample previously conveyed to us. I am confident that you will be pleased by the results. If the Denver Ore and Assay Company can be of further assistance, please do not hesitate to call upon us.

Very Cordially Yours,

Walter Grossberg

Lane unfolded and examined every page but could find nothing that resembled an assay report. There were old receipts, a bill of sale for some cattle, and a cost estimate to drill a water well. He replaced the contents and put the box in his bottom drawer.

The ruts bounced his pickup from side to side as Lane negotiated the two-lane driveway to Earl Wilson's ranch house. "You'd think the wealthiest man in the valley could pave his driveway," Lane muttered to himself as he slowed even more. Of course, it was classic Earl. He spent money on his livestock and his equipment, but little on comfort, his or anyone else's.

Lane parked and got out, stepping into a pack of Blue Heelers all vying for his attention. "Hello, Earl." He waved to Earl, who was coming out of the house. Lane had been meaning to make a social call on Earl to see if he had been satisfied with the leasing arrangement last summer. Earl had a big, easy smile on his face. "How're you, Lane?" He extended his big hand. "Good to see you. Come on in."

They traded light conversation for a while, his dogs, the weather, their leasing arrangement for next summer. Then Lane told him about the article and the letter he had found.

"I just assumed you knew all about Sven's disappearance," Earl said. "They never did find his body. Damnedest thing. The sheriff always believed foul play was involved, but he didn't have a bit of evidence."

"Any idea what the letter was about? The one about the missing assay report?"

Earl seemed to ponder this for a minute. "You know, there has always been a little bit of gold prospecting that goes on in the valley. There are credible reports of some occasional flakes from panning in Baker Creek. That was years ago though. And of course, the best story of all is the one about the Spanish finding a huge vein of gold and taking egg-sized nuggets out of a makeshift mine somewhere in the Spanish Peaks. The problem is anyone who finds anything is so secretive that it's hard to know the truth. There are a couple of locals who are believed to have a small mining operation somewhere that they sneak off to occasionally. I don't remember ever hearing anything about Sven even talking about gold though. If he had indeed sent a sample off to be assayed, though, you would think that he at least thought it was promising. I just don't know."

Earl continued with a mini geology lesson for Lane.

"Most of Colorado's serious gold deposits occur in a mineral belt extending southwest from central Boulder County through Chaffee and Gunnison counties. Most of the gold has been found on a line from North Clear Creek just west of Denver, Breckenridge, Alma and Fairplay, and Leadville. Gold was first discovered in Colorado in Arapahoe County in 1859. Since then, over forty million troy ounces have been mined. Hobby gold hunters still find it, but mostly along those historical sites."

Lane wondered how much his father had known about Sven's death. It was exasperating to think that his father was his only link to his past and he had been unwilling to share any of it.

Lane was intrigued. What was it that Sven sent to the Denver Ore and Assay Company? Where was the assay report and what did it contain?

He found Jerry Anderson in his real estate office in LaVeta. It was tough to show real estate during the dead of winter, and Jerry was glad to have the company. He listened to Lane with an occasional nod of the head.

"You know, I once showed a geology professor from Texas A&M several vacation cabins. He used to bring a group of students on a field trip to Cuchara every summer. He was fascinated with the valley and its rich history. I learned more than I needed to know about the geology of this place. Of course, you do know that coal mining was really big all over Huerfano County. Coal mining began sometime in the 1870s. You've gotta believe that if there was any hint of gold, someone would have found it and certainly tried to take it out of the ground. Anyway, back to the other professor. He believed that all the talk about gold probably got started by speculators trying to inflate the price of land by starting rumors based loosely on Bulls Eye mine, which is above the timber line on the other side of West Peak, and did yield some gold and silver many years ago. Gold does burn brighter in the imagination than coal. Who ever repeats romantic adventures about coal? Is it possible that someone panned gold from Baker Creek? Sure, but that's a long way from a rich vein of ore. All I ever heard about the Currys was that the old man, Sven, was a hardworking Swede. It doesn't sound likely that he would be caught up in chasing gold stories. As for the Spanish explorers, one of their enduring legacies is a rumor of Spanish gold."

Lane was perplexed. He began calling acquaintances in the academic world and came up with the name of a noted researcher in Colorado history who often wrote about the Spanish influence on Colorado. Dr. Jonathan Drake was associate professor of history at Colorado State University. He welcomed Lane into his home office on the outskirts of Fort Collins. It turned out that he was also a fly fisherman and fished at Blue Lake and Bear Lake in the summers.

Lane asked him about the enduring legend of Spanish gold around the Spanish Peaks.

"The Spanish explorers had specific mandates from the church in Mexico: gain a religious foothold in the new lands, civilize the natives, and become economically self-sufficient. In my opinion, they did not have the expertise or the manpower to engage in gold mining. The priests more than likely eked out a living farming and trading with the local Indians," Jonathan said.

"Do you have any historical maps of the Spanish trails and settlements in Southern Colorado?" Lane asked.

Jonathan thought for a minute.

"I traveled to Mexico City while researching my doctoral dissertation and got a look at some of the original maps brought back by Juan de Ulibarri in 1706. He is believed to be the first white man to travel to the Spanish Peaks via the Santa Fe Trail. The curators wouldn't let me photograph the hand-drawn maps, but I was able to draw reproductions. The Cucharas River has changed course over time, but the peaks and the dikes haven't changed, and would provide consistent landmarks relative to current maps. I assume that's what you have in mind?"

It was exactly what Lane had in mind, to translate the earliest Spanish maps into the context of the current landscape. Jonathan was intrigued by Lane's request and energized by Lane's probing questions. He agreed to superimpose the Spanish map onto a composite of the most recent topographical map of the Cuchara Valley.

Lane stopped in Golden on his way home to visit the Colorado School of Mines, one of the most prestigious engineering schools in the United States. It was a small, unpretentious campus, and he had no trouble finding the library. The school was also, as its name suggested—a mining school. Lane soon found what he was looking for, a reference to the Denver Ore and Assay Company. It seems the school had used them in the past to assay samples collected during various field trips. When he got home, he wrote a letter to them requesting that they search their records for a copy of the assay report sent to Sven Curry of Huerfano County, Colorado, sometime in 1880. He knew it was a long shot, but he felt compelled to find out all he could about Sven's death.

Lane and Steve both dreaded Christmas because it had always been Becky's favorite holiday. She *was* their Christmas spirit. She loved decorating the Christmas tree, and she loved the early-morning togetherness when they exchanged gifts.

It was Chris who invited them to ski in the Christmas Eve Torchlight Parade. "We need all the skiers we can corral to make it a really spectacular sight. Don't worry—we ski so slow that most of us keep our skis in a V. Just follow the skier in front of you and keep the flares straight out, perpendicular to your body while you rotate them clockwise. From the deck at Baker Creek, it looks like a sparkle parade snaking down the mountain."

They agreed. After all, most people never got to witness such a spectacular light show, much less be in one. Cold weather and additional snow had kept the base at a respectable sixty-five inches. The condos and local hotel were full, so there was an honest-to-goodness crowd to watch the torchlight parade. It was a magical experience for Lane. Skiing for the first time in the dark, the lights of the resort shimmering below and the stars shining above, the flares threw off an eerie glow across the snow as Lane glided silently down the mountain.

It was turning out to be one of the Timber's busiest nights of the season, and Mary was helping out. She had suggested they all meet at the Cuchara chapel for the 10:00 p.m. Christmas Eve service. The chapel was built in the late 1940s and was the site of numerous weddings as well as Sunday worship services. Without a resident pastor, the chapel relied on visiting ministers from a variety of denominations. Its simple architecture of logs and rock fit the site perfectly. The congregation viewed south through a large plate-glass window that framed the majestic fir trees and nearby peaks dominating the horizon. In late September and early October, the brilliant reds and yellows of the changing aspen leaves provided a startling kaleidoscope.

The chapel pews were filling up as Lane and Steve filed in. They took the first pew with room enough for them and Mary. Heavy snowflakes began to fall thickly, adding to the crusty white blanket on the ground. Mary found her way to their pew and slid between the two of them as the soloist began singing "Silent Night." She took a hand in each of her own and gently squeezed. The melody and lyrics surrounded them in a warm blanket of worship. For the first time since Becky's death, Lane felt at peace.

With the New Year well under way, Lane was immersed in preparations for the upcoming semester and set aside his quest for information about Sven's death and the "missing" assay report. In early February, he did receive a letter from Jonathan Drake, the Colorado state historian, including the topographical map Lane had left with him. The map was covered with markings, lines, and notations. The letter told Lane:

Lane,

Fascinating project you have here. Please keep me informed. I've marked up your topo map according to my hand-drawn map from Mexico City. It occurred to me that the Colorado portion of the "Spanish Trail" would tell only part of the story of how the trail was actually used. You probably need to know where the trail ended as well, so I've given you some notes on where the Spaniards traveled to after they left Colorado and where they traveled from when entering Colorado from other locales.

Cordially,
Jonathan

Lane was interested in one particular trail. He unfolded the map and took a few seconds to orient himself and make sure he was correctly interpreting Jonathan's markings. Jonathan was showing the primary trail used by the Spaniards that followed almost exactly the Cottonwood Canyon Trail, then merging into the Chaparral Trail, which ended at Apishapa Pass (currently Cordova Pass). Almost halfway between Apishapa Pass and where Cottonwood Canyon Trail intersected Highway 12 lay Chaparral Falls—the last place Sven Curry was thought to be before he disappeared.

PLAYING DIRTY

Chaparral Falls was a local scenic landmark—an actual waterfall in a fairly remote and hard-to-reach location on the Curry property. Hikers could reach it by taking off at Apishapa Pass and walking downhill. They could then back track to exit, but most were too exhausted by then and would exit on the Curry property. If it had involved a lot of foot traffic, Lane would be concerned, but there just weren't that many tourists who, first, knew about it or, second, were physically capable of the hike. So he had decided to be the gracious host to those few who panted their way across his property looking for the way out. The site was only reachable between late June and late September due to the snowfall anyway.

Was the confluence of the maps just some interesting historical trivia or did it mean something? How much had Sven known?

March, April, and May were usually months of hope—hope that spring was about to chase winter away, if only for a brief interlude. This year, they also ushered in activity, excitement, and distress for the Curry family.

It all started with a 7:00 a.m. knock on the front door. Lane and Steve were both on spring break from their respective schools but were both awake, just not expecting visitors.

"Mr. Curry?" the visitor apologetically asked when Lane opened the door. "I'm Don Campbell, water commissioner for Huerfano County. I apologize for the early visit, but I have a legal notice to deliver and I needed to make sure I caught you at your legal address." He handed Lane a fat brown envelope. "A legal action concerning your water rights has been filed with the Division 2 Water Court in Pueblo."

"A legal action. You mean a lawsuit?" Lane was dumbfounded.

"Not exactly. A party is asserting an 'abandonment of water rights' claim." Don continued, "Basically, a party is claiming that the water rights attached to this property have been abandoned because they have not been beneficially used or applied. I can't advise you because of my position, but you probably want to get a water attorney to explain this to you."

"Yes, I agree. Thanks." Lane began reading the first page of the packet of papers. *Great*, he thought, *the only thing more stupefying and arcane than lawyer's language has to be water-lawyer's language.*

The first call Lane made was to John Reynolds, district manager of the Cuchara Sanitation and Water Board. He was the most knowledgeable man in the valley where water was concerned. John agreed to meet at 10:00 a.m. in his office.

"I'm not an attorney, Lane, but I've been present in water court during numerous hearings and arguments," John said as he motioned Lane to a chair in front of his desk, "and I've done a lot of business with water attorneys." He opened the envelope and removed the stack of documents as he sat down. He read for several minutes, during which time he backtracked and reread several pages. Finally he looked up and addressed Lane.

"My initial reaction is that this is a nuisance claim. Number one, you've recently moved back onto the family property, and number two, you engaged in beneficial use last summer, well before this claim was filed, so it's obvious your intent was not a last-minute attempt to counteract this claim. My personal, nonlegal opinion is that you will prevail. However, you will have to defend your rights in court and that will take time and money."

"What possible reason would someone have to file a claim that has no chance of success?" Lane wondered out loud.

"I've seen numerous cases filed in water court as a diversion or as a negotiating tactic to confuse the real issue at hand. I know it's hard to believe, but there are lawyers who abuse the legal system including water court," John said sarcastically.

Lane left with a sick feeling, and he was thinking he needed to take a little time to sort this out before he did anything. He didn't realize how little time was left.

The phone was ringing when he walked into the house.

"Lane, this is Jerry Anderson. I've just received a written offer for your property from a broker in Denver. You probably should come up here and look at it."

Lane wanted to tell Jerry to just forget it—that he had more important things to worry about. The little voice in his head was protesting, though, so he climbed in his truck and headed back up the mountain.

Jerry was visibly agitated when Lane walked into his office.

"You're not going to believe this. Sit down."

Lane sat, confused at the eerie combination of anxiety and foolish grin on Jerry's face.

Jerry gushed, "In a nutshell, you've got an offer of five thousand dollars per acre plus four thousand dollars per WATER RIGHTS for a total of two million seven hundred fifty thousand dollars. What do you think?"

Lane was speechless.

"There's got to be a mistake somewhere," he muttered. Jerry handed him the offer letter and sat down himself. As the shock wore off, Lane began thinking again. "Who's making the offer?"

"I don't know. I've been so flustered I didn't even bother to look." Jerry began to read. "The offer is from the Panadero LLP at 13228 Durango Street in Denver."

Lane told him about the legal notice he had received that morning.

"This is too much of a coincidence," Lane said as he shook his head. "The claim on my water has to be a blatant attempt to intimidate me into selling the whole shebang. Or they're betting that I'll be overwhelmed by it all, especially the money, and be glad to be rid of the headache."

"They probably believe you're a disinterested owner of the family place and would be happy to have your inheritance in cash," Jerry said.

"I need to think about all this. Just sit on the offer. I'll get back to you," Lane shot over his shoulder as he exited the office.

Lane went to his office and closed the door. He needed to think, get some perspective. The one thing he was missing was information, so he sat down and read the legal notice word for word. It wasn't until he had read the cover letter the second time that something caught his attention. At the very bottom of the page in small print was the address of the law firm filing the claim, *13228 Durango St. Denver, Colorado*—the address of Panadero LLP, the wannabe buyer of the Curry property. "Well, that's no surprise," thought Lane. He had assumed there was a connection. There was one other dot that begged to be connected, but he kept coming up short. The timing—what was it about the timing?

Steve's response was predictable. "We're not going to sell, are we?"

Lane reassured Steve. He then planned his strategy.

Jerry recommended a young attorney in Walsenburg over more experienced, established lawyers in Denver.

"Robert Gonzales is the smartest lawyer I've ever met. He's not only a lawyer, he has a master's degree in hydrology. He is young, but he is fearless, and I promise you he won't be intimidated by anyone. Talk to him and you'll see what I mean."

Lane trusted Jerry's judgment, so he called Robert and made an appointment. He also knew Jerry was discreet.

"I need a private investigator," he told Jerry.

"Umm, let me think about that. I'll call you later."

The next morning, Jerry called Lane. "I found this guy a rental cabin a couple of summers ago. His name is Mark Garrett. He owns a small private firm in Denver that specializes in investigating corporate espionage. He was a diplomatic security service agent for most of his career. I hired him when I suspected a potential buyer was trying to run a scam on me. He can do it all: surveillance, technology, backgrounds, skip tracing, interrogations—you name it."

It took Mark a couple of days to call back, and when he did, he got right to the point.

"Lane, I always do background checks on potential clients before we get too far into their problem. Do I have your permission?"

Lane didn't hesitate. "Check away and call me when you're ready."

Mark told him to send him copies of all the documents he had and a written outline of what he wanted, a timeline of events and a list of names and positions of the people involved. He said he would get back to Lane within the week.

Very efficient and to the point, Lane thought. I like that.

Lane's next stop was Robert Gonzales's office. He had already sent him the legal notice. They shook hands and Lane sat down.

"Mr. Curry, there's no question that we can successfully defend your water rights and defeat this claim. My number one priority is to meet all the submittal requirements of the court in a timely manner so we don't lose by default. That won't be a problem. I also believe that your beneficial use and your intent to continue beneficial use will suffice in court. To that end, we'll need a deposition or direct testimony from Earl Wilson."

Lane agreed to provide all the receipts and construction contracts for remodeling the house, the grass lease from last summer, and his employment contract with the university, all to demonstrate his intent to remain in the family house and to use the water rights. He also showed Robert the real estate offer and gave his opinion about the relationship of the purchase offer and the water court claim.

Robert laughed. "Very interesting." He promised to keep Lane informed of every move.

Lane felt energized. All of his soldiers were in place and working. He reveled in the intricacy of the situation and the prospect of the intellectual battle ahead. His first step was to get more information about them than they had about him. The little voice in his head kept nagging him: *there's more here than meets the eye.* Lane listened carefully.

Mark Garrett called a week later. He wanted to come to Cuchara and meet with Lane to update him, plus he wanted to walk around Lane's place and "get a feel for the property." He rented a condo and agreed to meet Lane at the Timbers at 7:30 the next morning. The restaurant was closed, but Joe and Ernie were cleaning and doing minor repairs as they prepared to open on Mother's Day. They were glad to let Lane and Mark use a corner table and drink cup after cup of hot coffee.

Mark began, "I've discovered a family tree you might be interested in. You had a sharp eye when you noticed the address of the law firm matched the address of Panadero, LLP. But you missed another connection. Look at the law firm's name."

"Atkinson, Grossberg, Hamilton, and Hughes," Lane read out loud. "Well, I'll be damned." He looked at Mark. "I'm betting you already know if this Grossberg is related to the Grossberg of the Denver Ore and Assay Company." Mark was smiling.

"Yes, indeed. This one is Albert Grossberg, the sixty-year-old son of Matthew Grossberg. Matthew founded the law firm in 1945. He died ten years ago when he was eighty-six years old. Albert is now the managing partner of the firm. Matthew was born in 1895 to Walter and Ida Grossberg. Walter was the owner of the Denver Ore and Assay Company. That firm went out of business in 1950 when Walter died. Since then, all correspondence to the Assay Company has been forwarded to the law firm.

"Attention: Albert Grossberg. There's no question that your letter requesting information about Sven Curry's sample ended up in Albert's hands."

"And Panadero, LLP?" Lane asked.

"The general partner of Panadero is a corporation recently incorporated as Chaparral Incorporated. Grossberg is listed as the CEO. The directors are all partners in the law firm. It's not a very elegant veil but would hide the relationships to the casual observer."

Lane was soaking it all in, trying to make sense of it.

Mark sat back and sipped his coffee as he let Lane think for a minute. He knew about Lane's credentials. Mark always checked out his clients before he accepted a job. He even read one of Lane's academic articles. Lane liked to get right to the point. He often connected disparate dots, usually in unconventional ways, to arrive at elegant solutions to problems.

"There's more."

Lane leaned forward. "What?"

"In 1960, ten years after Walter died, his son Matthew bought a cabin in Cuchara. He gifted it to his son Albert in 1980. Five years later, Albert remodeled and enlarged the cabin. It's on Aspen Road. Let's go take a look." Mark had surmised that Lane was an action guy, not reckless, but action-oriented. He also wanted to get Lane out of a public place so they could talk in absolute privacy.

Since Lane knew his way around he drove. Mark continued what was turning out to be his first report even though they had not signed a contract for services.

"One interesting item about the remodeled and expanded house is that Albert had a wall safe installed."

Lane looked at him. "How could you know that?"

"Easy. They had to get a building permit for that scope of remodeling job, and those are kept in the codes and compliance office at the Huerfano County Courthouse. They're public records. Plus, the contractor had to submit as-built drawings before the county would issue the certificate of occupancy, also a public record. And it's not just any safe. It's from Industrial Safe and Lock Company in Denver. They only do very high-end safes. Albert must keep something very special in that house."

Lane turned onto Aspen Road. It was remote and unpaved, like all the roads in Cuchara. The south side of the road bordered national forest land, providing the owners with virtually unlimited back yards.

"There it is." Mark pointed to the left. "Slow down." He did a quick assessment of the surroundings, including the other houses. "Where does this road lead?"

"Up to the Cuchara water plant. It basically dead-ends there."

It was a traditional log/rock house with lots of windows and a wraparound covered porch. The back of the house was built into the sloping lot, and the front was perched solidly on large cedar piers.

"I'm thinking that Sven's assay report is in this house and that we need to see it," Mark said. "He would want that report with him when he was here, and he wouldn't want to carry it back and forth. My guess is that Walter accidentally left the report out of the envelope he mailed to Sven. That was about the time that Sven disappeared, so he never inquired about it. It fell into Matthew's hands and ultimately, maybe when Matthew died, Albert came to own it. It doesn't really matter how he got it, I'm betting that Albert has it and has been making trips down here plotting a strategy to own the land. Your arrival, and especially your inquiry, must have really rattled him and forced him into a knee-jerk response. Lane, we need to see Sven's assay report."

The little voice in Lane's head shrieked. They rode in silence. Mark didn't push. He wanted to give Lane plenty of room on this. It would be breaking and entering, and just because it was the property of a thief (or his grandson) wouldn't carry much weight in court. Of course he could protect Lane—and himself. The house would be a breeze, and the county law enforcement was at least forty-five minutes away under the best circumstances. But a person like Lane would not agree to participate in criminal activity lightly—even from afar.

"When do you leave?" Lane asked.

"Right after you give me a tour of your property. Then we need to move quickly. I don't want to rush you, but I know you see the need to get out ahead of him."

As Lane drove Mark around the property, he told him all about Sven, the research on the Spanish trails, and he oriented him with a current topographical map. They got out briefly where the Cottonwood Canyon Trail entered the property. There would be too much snow on the ground for them to hike to Chaparral Falls. Mark made a few notes but mostly listened to Lane for the hour-long session. As he prepared to leave, he gave Lane an expectant glance. Lane knew what he wanted.

"I'll call you tomorrow with my decision," Lane said as he extended his hand.

DECISION TIME

Lane had been supremely confident up to this point. He had felt in command of the situation; it was familiar territory, complete with a variety of known and unknown variables to factor into the decision-making process. The only difference was, instead of plotting strategy and formulating action steps for a client, he was the advisor *and* the client. It was also so easy to advise others on what to do and how to do it, to glibly quote the probabilities and expected values of each course of action, to patiently urge them down a certain path. It was a big difference. This time, he would have to bear the consequences. Even more importantly, Steve would also bear the consequences, perhaps for years after Lane was gone.

He was, in theory and in practice, a very honest man. He had taught Steve, by pronouncement and by example, to always do the ethical thing. Steve's questions, such as, "But Dad, what if you don't know the ethical thing to do? What if there is more than one ethical choice?" went right to the heart of most ethics quandaries. Lane would then likely quote some of the often-used recipes: above all, do no harm; being ethical means doing the right thing when no one is looking, and when faced with the conundrum of more than one ethical course of action (or lack thereof), ask which one will do the least harm. After these obligatory platitudes, Lane would tell him that we lived in a world of shifting values and ever-changing lines between society's version of what's right and wrong. Most of our daily decisions embodied our core values. We had to be in touch with those core values, and we had to constantly protect them from the daily onslaught of negativism and spiritual corruption that pervaded our society. Once you really understood your core values, they would always show up for the moral battle. You can't suppress them, even if you try. They define how you act and react, usually without your even being aware of them.

So, what to do? Lane's ethical choice involved no shades of gray; it was starkly black and white. Would he participate in a break-in and possible theft of documents that belonged to his family? As Lane would speak to a client, the little voice in his head spoke plainly and to the point, "It's illegal. The question is, are you willing to do something illegal?" It wasn't a question of getting caught.

He knew that Mark could accomplish the break-in undetected. Could Lane live with it? He spent most of that night deciding.

He would tell Mark not to remove anything from the cabin so he would not be committing theft. Lane decided breaking into the cabin to right a decades-old wrong against his family was ethically justified if not legally justified. The amount of harm would be minimal and he could live with it.

"Hello." Lane was taken aback when Mark answered the first ring at 7:05 a.m. the next morning.

"Mark, this is Lane. Let's do it."

"All right. I'll call you when I'm done." He didn't volunteer the date or time or anything else about his plan.

Mark knew the nightly schedule of Huerfano County deputies. Once every two nights, a deputy would drive through Cuchara Valley. If the Dog Bar was open, the deputy would drive through Cuchara on the one and only street and maybe stop and walk into the Dog Bar to check for underage drinkers. Mark would work on the night not covered by the roving deputy. He also chose a moonless night. Even though there was a dense stand of trees that crowded the Grossbeck's house, he wanted every possible advantage. He would use night-vision equipment once in the house to avoid any light that could be spotted from a wayward driver.

He parked his car at the entrance to the Spring Creek picnic area and headed up the adjacent hill at a brisk pace. After hiking almost two hours, he came to the back of the Grossbeck lot and within one hundred feet of the back of the house. He waited in the deep shadows and watched for any sign of movement. He had actually knocked on the front door earlier that day to see if anyone was around. The property manager of the house had told him none of the owners were scheduled to be here, but Mark wanted to be extra careful. It was almost 2:00 a.m., and Mark started his final descent down the slope, moving from tree to tree and pausing momentarily behind each one.

He quickly disabled the alarm system and was through the outside garage door. The interior door to the house was no obstacle either, and he soon had the night-vision goggles on as he headed for the master bedroom. From the as-built house plans he had examined at the county, he knew the safe was in the wall at the east end of the walk-in closet. The safe was more of a challenge, but he had it open after fifteen minutes. He turned on a small light, knowing that it could not be seen from outside.

After meticulously looking at each document, he lay them to the side, careful to keep them in the same order. He pulled out a small metal box and raised the lid. There was a piece of paper housed in a plastic protective sleeve. Leaving the document in the sleeve, he aimed his light so he could read it. The paper was very fragile, and the cursive writing was tiny and pinched.

THE PAST MEETS THE PRESENT

It was a letter to Mr. Sven Curry residing in Spanish Peaks. The opening sentence was illegible. There was a list, though, that had been written in darker letters.

8 escudos
27.0 grams
1.5 inches dia
22 ct
92% pure

The closing sentences were illegible as well. Mark wrote down the information and returned the antique letter to its box. He didn't want them to know anyone had been in their house. As he laid the plastic sleeve on the bottom of the metal box, his hand brushed against a velvet pouch with a drawstring. He picked it up. Mark could feel a hard round object through the velvet. It seemed heavy for its size. He removed his gloves to more easily handle it and then removed a gold coin. Not wanting to waste time here wondering what it was or what it meant, he hastily sketched both sides of the coin, being careful to record every single word, symbol, and numeral as close to actual size as he could. He returned the coin to the bag, put the bag back in the box, and reconstructed the safe's contents to their original state. Then he drove straight to Denver.

Spanish escudo

Once Lane had made his decision, he was at peace. He would just live with it. There was only one person he would ever share this with. He knocked on the door to Mary's studio. The Timbers wouldn't open for several weeks, and Mary was spending every daylight hour in her studio.

"Well, hello stranger." She welcomed Lane with a beaming smile. "I'm glad you're still around."

Lane went in and smiled sheepishly. "I'm sorry I haven't come by sooner, but it's been a very interesting and busy couple of weeks." Mary could sense the seriousness in his voice and his demeanor. She put down her brush and focused on him and his story. He told her everything, including his decision to have Mark search for documents in the Grossbeck house. She listened intently, in silence, broken only by "Wow!" when she heard the offer for his property. When he finished, he leaned back in his chair and looked at her expectantly. She knew exactly what her role was.

"It sounds to me like you're in a win-win situation. A stressful one to be sure, but all the possible outcomes are good. If you sell the family property, you and Steve will reap a financial windfall. If you keep it, you'll continue to live in a place you both love. If you lose the water rights, I assume they will have to pay you for them, right? Even if you don't ever find out what happened to Sven, you won't be any worse off than you are now." Mary was careful not to inject any judgment in her soliloquy. She put her hand over his.

Lane smiled. What a beautiful version of the Lane Curry technique. He relaxed.

He called Robert Gonzalez to check on his water case.

"I'm submitting our response next week. It will take the court at least a month to schedule the first hearing. I'll call you as soon as they do. Our strategy is to go as slow as possible and drag it out as long as we can. We want to tire out the claimants."

It had been two weeks since he had seen Mark, but he knew Mark would call him just as soon as he knew something.

Actually, Mark showed up at his door the next morning.

They sat at the kitchen table, and Lane poured coffee for both of them.

"First, I did find Grossbeck's assay report to Sven. But it wasn't a typical assay report. I also found this." He showed him a color drawing of the gold coin.

"This coin was in the same box as the assay report."

Lane held the drawing up and peered at it.

"What is it?"

"It's a Spanish gold coin, minted in Spain and sent to the New World to help finance expeditions and the establishment of the church. I'm pretty sure this is what Sven sent to be assayed. He didn't know what else to do with it. How did he get it? I don't know. Was it related to his disappearance? The numismatist, after seeing my drawing and the information from the assay report, told me that this is an eight escudos coin weighing twenty-seven grams. It's ninety-two percent pure, which equates to twenty-two-carat gold. Today, these coins bring anywhere from one thousand five hundred dollars to two thousand dollars each at auction. Now the question is, are there more of them?"

The only other details of his late-night excursion Mark shared with Lane was that he did not remove any of the contents of Grossberg's safe. Mark left the drawing and the notes from the assay report. Lane thanked him and told him he would let him know how it all turned out.

Lane decided to visit Jonathan personally at Colorado State University and called for an appointment. Two days later, he was in Jonathan's office.

"Jonathan, what are the chances that the Spanish transported gold coins through the Spanish Peaks area?" Lane placed the drawing on his desk.

"Ah, gold bullion," Jonathan said. "Not too many of these around."

Lane had decided that he needed to trust the historian, so he told him about the coin they believed Sven had sent off to be assayed and the resulting report.

"It wouldn't be hard to imagine that the Spanish carried lots of these to their struggling churches for financial support. It took many of them years to become financially independent, and many of them never did. Mexico City had to furnish them with hard currency.

"You know, the literature is rife with stories of lost treasure, and some of the stories or legends or whatever you want to call them involve Southern Colorado. There's the story of Purgatory Canyon and the Humana and Bonilla expedition of 1539, which passed near Trinidad. Twelve chests of gold coins were hidden, so the story goes. La Caverna del Oro is a colorful story of a gold mine situated thirteen thousand feet up Marble Mountain near Westcliff and mined in the fifteenth century. So the location is very central to some of the enduring legends. Of course, none of it has ever been found. Yes, it's possible that the Spanish moved gold through that area."

Jonathan paused for a minute. "I don't think there's any way to narrow down beyond that what the Spanish were doing in that particular region. There's just not enough of a record."

CHAPARRAL FALLS

Lane knew he was right. He had been grasping for straws. While Lane was driving south on I-25 headed for home, Steve was preparing for his first extended hike of the spring. His dad had told him about Sven and the Spanish maps and Chaparral Falls. It didn't take much to launch Steve on a wilderness hike, but the idea of his great-great-grandfather disappearing among the ghosts of a Spanish expedition fired his imagination. He had never been to Chaparral Falls, so this was the perfect excuse. Find Sven! He planned to leave early in the morning.

Lane had decided to give himself a day off from thinking about water court, the offer, the gold coin, and Sven. He was going to spend the day with Mary. There was nothing more he could do anyway. He had instructed Jerry to simply ignore the real estate offer. Robert was using every delaying tactic known to the legal profession to frustrate the water claim. He had accepted that he would probably never know what happened to Sven.

He watched Steve with the particular wonder that comes over every father when he realizes his child has crossed over into young adulthood. Steve was packing a backpack with water, lunch (for him and Sampson), his routine first-aid kit, and emergency items such as a flashlight, matches in a waterproof container, a high-tech thermal blanket, and a compass. He had become quite the outdoors expert, knowledgeable in basic survival, including survival first aid. He had even spent a night out with Chris in a snow cave that they constructed in the middle of winter. Chris was adamant that Steve experience it firsthand so he would have confidence that he could survive in a desperate situation. Many lost climbers, hikers, and skiers died simply because they lost hope. A degree of knowledge and self-confidence had saved many a lost or injured hiker.

Sampson was standing outside the back door, obviously agitated. He had spotted Steve with his backpack and knew that they were about to embark somewhere. He could not contain his excitement. Jumping stiff-legged into the air and barking were Steve's signals to hurry up.

"Mary's going to pick me up at ten, and we're going to Pueblo for the day," Lane reminded Steve. He had no reservations leaving Steve behind with Sampson.

Steve was the most responsible person he knew, and there was no better guardian than Sampson.

"Okay, Sampson and I will be at Chaparral Falls or on the trail between here and there. I want to spend some time poking around up there, but we'll be back before dark."

Lane hugged him and repeated the age-old parent admonition to "be careful." It was late May, and the Cucharas River was higher than Steve had ever seen it. The winter's record snowfall was now melting high in the mountains and pouring downstream. He and Sampson stopped on the ancient wooden bridge and watched the river rush and swirl beneath them with a loud roar. The trees closed in around them as they proceeded on the trail that was growing steeper by the minute. Patches of snow lingered in the shade, and Sampson rolled in most of them and then shook the icy flakes from his fur. He would disappear briefly, but Steve could hear him crashing through the undergrowth as Sampson pursued an array of interesting scents. Sampson was definitely not a stealth dog.

Chaparral Falls

Steve could hear the waterfall before he could see it and was disappointed when it finally came into view. His imagination had painted a picture of a steep cliff hundreds of feet tall with a booming wall of water plummeting to the ground. Its height was more like twenty or thirty feet. The water was flowing very fast, swollen by the runoff of melting snow but was quite tame and only about fifteen feet wide. It splashed into a small pool before it continued its rush to the river. A level clearing measuring approximately 150 feet in diameter punctuated the steep terrain. Steve could see where the trail exited the clearing on the other side and continued its climb to Apishapa Pass. His disappointment was fleeting as he took in the solitude and beauty of the spot. Sampson lapped water from the pool and plopped down where Steve was rummaging through his backpack. He doled out treats to Sampson and ate his sandwich. His seated position allowed him to view the waterfall from the side, and he noticed that due to the inward slope of the rock wall, he could actually look between the falling water and the seemingly solid rock backdrop. The pool appeared to be a couple of feet deep in the middle. Watching the falling water cascade into the pool, he could see that it first crashed into a narrow outcropping, which caused most of the spray. He guessed that in periods of less volume, the lip would be well above the surface of the pool.

"What is it, Sampson?"

The dog's gaze was fixated on the far side of the clearing. Normally, he would respond to Steve's voice by looking at him and wagging his tail, always eager for attention. Instead, he slowly rose into a crouching position and froze there. His upper lip was now curled in a grimace. Steve could hear a deep, guttural noise in Sampson's throat. It sent shivers down his spine.

Steve slowly stood up and swept his vision back and forth across the jumble of fallen aspen trees and underbrush that surrounded the clearing. Nothing. Then a slight movement from a stand of tall dead grass caught his eye.

Steve's heart froze in midbeat. He was instantly deaf and blind to the world, save for that one spot that his mind was fighting to comprehend. His breathing became shallow and labored. His heart was now pounding. It felt like a jackhammer in his chest.

The mountain lion stood up in one fluid motion and silently looked around. He was a good three feet tall at the shoulder and at least seven feet long. His tail added another two to three feet of length as it twitched left to right. He was a beautiful golden creature. His head was huge.

Was he hunting or had he just happened upon them and needed to satisfy his curiosity?

Mountain Lion (Puma concolor)

"Easy, boy." Steve reached down to grab Sampson's collar to restrain him. If Steve did not bolt and run, there might be a chance the big cat would decide they were not his prey. Running would seal Steve's fate. For a brief moment, Steve shared a sense with all other creatures that had stood before a predator, a desperate feeling of inevitable doom.

Steve was panic stricken. He avoided eye contact with the cat and slowly turned his head to look toward the waterfall. He didn't know what else to do. Slowly, ever so slowly, he inched backward toward the falling water. Maybe if he and Sampson could get behind the wall of falling water, the cat would be discouraged. Cats didn't like water, right? He doubted if that held true for a mountain lion on the hunt. Maybe the combination of the noise and splashing water would be enough. Another step backward. Careful. He must not slip on the rocks.

The big cat's posture seemed almost nonchalant, so Steve allowed himself a sliver of hope. Back one more step now. Sampson was hard to maneuver. Steve was applying as much force as he could from a standing position with his right knee bent, but Sampson was not cooperating.

"Easy, Sampson. Easy." They moved back slightly. Suddenly, the cat fixated on them with a wide-eyed stare and crouched low to the ground. He advanced one silent step at a time. His stride was huge. Steve knew that if he charged, it would be a matter of seconds before he would be on them. The cat crept forward one more step then raised his head slightly and tensed. He had crossed an invisible line. Sampson lunged free and tore after the cat before Steve could react. He could never have held him anyway. Steve knew he could do nothing but try to save himself. He managed to get on the narrow lip of rock and began to inch into the water fall, pressing his back against the wall. He crept toward the center where the waterfall seemed to be the heaviest. Thankfully, he could hear nothing of the violent encounter. The water was ice cold and would numb his hands and feet before too long. He had his hands splayed out to either side of his body for balance as he continued to move sideways to his right. Suddenly, he felt a crevice in the wall. He stuck his hand into the opening. It was almost as tall as he was. The bottom seemed to be just above the pool's surface. He slid his right shoulder through it and then his hip. He was now holding onto the inside of the wall and, with a push from his left foot, was able to squeeze his entire body through. All sound became muffled, and the darkness covered all but a slice of light escaping through the sheet of water.

The cat was surprised by Sampson's speed and by the fact that Sampson was running *at* him instead of *away* from him. That had never happened before. The surprise slowed the cat's response a split second, allowing Sampson to hit the cat broadside with 115 pounds of fury. The cat rolled and Sampson was on him, tearing at him with what must have seemed like a buzz saw of teeth. Even though the cat outweighed Sampson by at least eighty pounds, he was deceptively quick. He righted himself in one supple movement, momentarily rose up on his hind legs, and sent a giant right paw crashing into Sampson's shoulder. Luckily, the cat's claws were only partially extended, so Sampson sustained more of a blunt trauma than a slashing. The blow sent him skidding and rolling across the ground, and the cat was on him before Sampson could regain his footing. Sampson rolled onto his back, and his powerful hind legs saved his life as he pushed the cat off before he could get to Sampson's throat. Sampson was bleeding from the initial blow. The cat circled Sampson, watching for a sign of weakness. Sampson surprised the cat again. He charged him head on. The cat sprung straight into the air but was slightly off balance, and Sampson clipped his right flank, flipping the cat over onto his back. Sampson reversed direction and was on him in a fury of slashing and gnashing teeth, tearing chunks out of his skin. Surprise was Sampson's ally again. The cat responded furiously but a split second too slowly. Sampson found the big cat's throat and fiercely planted the full force of his huge jaws on the cat's lifeline. The cat responded with a ferocity found only in fights to the death. He dug his hind claws into Sampson's belly and writhed violently. Sampson bit down harder and held his ground, sensing his foe's death was at hand.

Steve slipped out of the cave and tried to peer through the falling water. He could see vague motionless shapes on the ground and inched his way back along the rim to solid ground. He thought Sampson and the cat were dead. He approached with a growing sense of dread. Soon he was sure the cat was dead.

"Sampson," he whispered. Sampson was soaked in blood. "Sampson." He reached out and touched Sampson's head. At his touch, Sampson's tail flickered.

"Oh, God."

He maneuvered so he could see where Sampson was bleeding and was shocked at the carnage. He stroked his head. "You can let go, Sampson." Sampson held the cat's throat tight as if he was still protecting Steve. Steve straddled Sampson on his knees and pulled his jaws apart. He could feel Sampson's weak breath as he wheezed. His eyes were open but glazed.

Steve didn't know what to do. How was he going to save Sampson? The bleeding. I've got to stop the bleeding. In a panic, he started pulling up dead grass and scooped up handfuls of mud from the banks of the small pool and mashed them together into a yellow and black stringy paste. He spread the mixture over Sampson's underbelly until it was covered. He opened up his first-aid kit, took out the one measly roll of gauze, and began wrapping Sampson's midsection, trying to bind the makeshift bandage to his wound. Next, he took off his jacket and fit it around Sampson's belly and tied the arms together tightly so that they applied pressure to the wounds. He took off his belt and tightened that around the jacket to provide another source of pressure.

He got down on his knees and put his head close to Sampson's ear.

"Can you hear me, Sampson? I'm going to get you down the mountain and you're going to be all right. You've got to trust me."

Steve began sobbing. "Sampson, you can't die on me."

"God, you've got to help me save Sampson. He saved my life. I know you want him to live. I just know it. Now you've got to give me the strength to get him down."

The collar of Steve's jacket was right behind Sampson's ears. Steve unzipped the collar and unrolled the hood. He used the hood as a handle and began pulling Sampson. He needed something more substantial to hold onto. Remembering all the old movies about cowboys and Indians he had watched with his dad, he found two fairly straight, small aspen trees. Using his hunting knife, he cut them down and skinned off the branches. He cut them again so that they were both about six feet long. He cut the straps off his back pack, split it, and used the material along with the straps and small pieces of fiberglass rope he carried in his pack to fashion a web using the two aspen trees to support both sides. He then laid it down flat and pulled Sampson onto the web. Now he could hold one aspen tree in each hand and pull the makeshift stretcher to make much better time.

He checked Sampson one more time. He then started out on the longest journey of his young life.

It was close to 3:30 by the time Steve started down the mountain. Darkness came much sooner in the mountains as the sun dropped behind the highest peak well before the day was done.

Mary and Lane pulled into the driveway about 4:00 p.m. She helped him carry some packages in so she could tell Steve hello.

"Well, I expected him home by now," Lane said as he looked out the kitchen window toward the old wooden bridge. "He must be on his way."

At 5:00 p.m., Lane was worried. He called Mary to tell her he was setting out on foot to look for Steve. He wanted someone to know what direction he was going. He took the big flashlight, put on his heavy coat, and headed toward the trail.

Steve was exhausted. The cumulative stress and physical exertion were taking their toll on him. The moon was out, so he could at least see the trail, but the tension of needing to walk slowly to not cause more bleeding and the need to get Sampson to the vet right away was wearing him down. Then he thought he saw a light flicker below.

"Steve!" Then after a few seconds, "Steve!"

"Dad, I'm up here." He could barely get the words out. He started flicking his flashlight to get his dad's attention.

After making sure Steve was not injured, Lane sent him to the house to get the truck and bring it to the bridge. He would finish pulling Sampson down the mountain.

They hoisted Sampson into the back and stopped briefly at the house where Lane called David Medford, the vet, to meet them at his office. During the drive, Steve was able to tell Lane the outline of what had happened. It was obvious to Lane that Steve was in shock or something close to it.

David met them at the clinic just outside LaVeta. Lane tried to get Steve to leave with him and go to the hospital to get checked out. Steve would have none of it. He would get close to hysteria if Lane pushed the subject. Two hours after arriving at the vet's, David came out.

"I got him cleaned up and stitched up. He's getting a transfusion now, and I'm pumping antibiotics into him. Your homemade bandages probably saved his life. He surely would have bled to death on the trip down the mountain without those. He may not make it through the night though. He's really torn up, and he lost a lot of blood. You just need to be prepared." David was speaking directly to Steve. "You did everything you possibly could." He patted Steve on the shoulder.

"I want to stay with him tonight," Steve said shakily.

"Steve, we need to get you to the doctor too. There's nothing else you can do here," Lane said softly.

"Dad, he saved my life." Steve's voice was breaking and tears were welling up. "Don't you understand?"

David interrupted, "Lane, I'll get Doc Billington to come over here and take a look at Steve. If he's worried, then we can figure something out. I've got a cot we can set up in a heartbeat and let Steve sleep here. I'm gonna be coming over every two hours to check on Sampson anyway." He took Lane's elbow and walked him slowly out to the waiting room. "I'm pretty sure that Steve's suffering from a mild case of shock, which won't get any better if we make him leave and go to the hospital. Doc can sedate him, and we can get some food in him and let him sleep here. He'll be much more likely to respond to treatment if he's not upset about leaving."

He continued, "And you know I've seen some amazing things happen between a man and his animal. It just might make the difference for Sampson if Steve stays close by."

Lane nodded and thanked David for his help and concern.

"Steve, you can stay here tonight if you'll agree to eat some food. I'll get you something from the Timbers. Oh, and you have to let Doc Billington look at you when he gets here. Deal?"

"Deal. Thanks, Dad."

Lane hugged his son. "I'll be back soon with some food."

Lane drove to the Timbers where Joe fixed Steve's favorite hamburger. Lane explained to Mary what had happened and told her that he would also stay at the vet's clinic tonight. He didn't want to leave his family alone.

Steve took the sedative that Doc gave him, plus lots of fluids with his meal. He devoured the hamburger and was soon fast asleep.

Doc told Lane that, physically, Steve was fine, mostly exhausted from his ordeal.

David called Ronnie Evans, the game warden, and told him about Steve's experience. Ronnie said he would go up there the next day and perform a field autopsy on the big cat. "That's one lucky young man," he said.

Lane woke early and drove into LaVeta to bring breakfast back for both of them. He also brought fresh coffee for David.

"He held his own during the night, so that's a good sign. It's still touch and go, though," David reported to them.

"Can I see him"? Steve asked.

"Sure"

Mary showed up while Steve was visiting Sampson and got an update from Lane. When Steve came out, Mary put her arms around him and squeezed him tight. Steve just couldn't hold it anymore. He broke down and sobbed. His body heaved in Mary's embrace. "Mary, he . . . he saved my life. I can't let him die." He sobbed uncontrollably for a few minutes, all the time holding on to Mary.

"I know, I know," was all she said. When he had calmed down, he told them both what had happened. Lane and Mary listened in silence, humbled by their brush with death.

They repeated the same routine that night. Lane was not willing to leave Steve after such a close call. David woke them both up at 5:00 a.m.

"It's good news. Sampson made some good progress. I'm pretty sure now that he's going to recover. There's no sign of infection, and that's what I thought would kill him."

Once Sampson turned the corner, he recovered rapidly, and they took him home after ten days. He slept in Steve's room for another week. The only residue from his encounter with the mountain lion seemed to be his tendency to cling to Steve whenever they were together. When they went on walks, Sampson wouldn't roam out ahead and to the sides like in the past. He would walk close to Steve and lay down at his feet when Steve stopped.

Lane had decided he would go to Chaparral Falls and examine the cave behind the falls. He and Steve were concerned about how Sampson would react to the scene. In the end, they decided that Steve would remain behind with Sampson. Lane and Mary would ride to the falls on horseback. Lane packed two large flashlights, kerosene lantern, and his only firearm, a bolt action 30.06.

Their trip to the falls was uneventful. The game warden had removed the lion's body. Lane tied the horses and left their saddles on because he did not expect to be long. They each took a flashlight, and Lane carried the lantern. Steve had described the journey behind the water fall, so they waterproofed the lantern and matches. It was early June, and the volume of water coming over the falls had not diminished. They crept along the rock lip with their backs to the wall. Lane went first and found the cleft in the wall. He squeezed through, holding the lantern above his head where there was slightly more room. He held his hand out to guide Mary and help her keep her balance as she contorted her body to slip into the dark cavern. Lane flicked on his flashlight and handed it to Mary. He struck a match and held it to the wick of the lantern. The cavern was illuminated by its soft light. They stood silent for several minutes, wondering how long it had been since the room had seen light.

The room was irregular in shape but appeared to be about forty feet long and maybe thirty feet wide. The walls curved inward as they rose to converge at the apex approximately fifteen feet above the floor. The cave's floor was solid rock and was partially covered with rubble of various sizes. The walls and floor were damp, although there was no visible dripping. Lane put the lantern down in the center and played the flashlight beam across the back wall. He had been mistaken. The back wall did not end where he thought. It continued to the left as it defined a passageway. The light revealed a pile of rubble blocking the way, but there was additional space beyond. Lane climbed to the top of the pile and shone his light beyond. He could see piles of something, not rubble but material that appeared more orderly than simply fallen rock.

They worked for two hours, tossing rocks, most of which were no bigger than apples. Lane had scrutinized the ceiling just above the rock pile and could see no signs of impending collapse. Now they could walk through the narrow hallway into the rest of the cavern. Lane held the lantern out in front and led the way, carefully choosing his footing among the rubble. The hallway was about ten feet in length and led to another opening. As they were about to step into this back room, Lane heard Mary suck in her breath.

"Lane, look here!"

He turned to where her flashlight beam was pointing and saw a flash of white. It seemed to be shining back at them, a bright spot in the darkness. They both kneeled. Lane put the lantern down and moved several rocks.

It was a human skull. They carefully moved more rocks and uncovered what remained of the skeleton.

"Do you think it's Sven?" Mary asked.

"I don't know," he said as he stood and moved further into the room with the lantern. "I just don't know." His voice seemed to be coming from a faraway place. Mary stood up and stepped toward him. The back room was bathed in light.

"Oh my God!" Mary couldn't breathe for a second.

Sven's secret

The back room was full of ancient leather bags, most of them falling apart, their contents spilling onto the floor. Lane picked up one of the bags and it fell apart. The rotting bags were stacked chest high and fifteen deep along the back wall, which was almost twenty feet long. The bags seemed to flash and wink back at them as they aimed the flashlight beams through the darkness. Lane picked up a handful of coins and spread them out in Mary's outstretched hands.

"There really is such a thing as lost treasure," he whispered.

They only brought a handful of coins back with them. The three of them, Lane, Steve, and Mary stayed up almost all night drinking coffee and discussing what to do next. Lane did not want to "exhume" Sven (if it even was Sven). He believed it was him and could not imagine what could be served by having DNA tests conducted to verify it. For what purpose? If it was not Sven, what then? How many archeologists does it take to ruin a perfectly peaceful resting place? No, he would let the deceased rest, and he would continue to believe that it was Sven, who had probably discovered the cave by accident and had just been there at the wrong time. Mary and Steve agreed that some family secrets are better left untold.

What about the gold coins? They were worth millions—of that Lane was sure. What would be the aftermath of the windfall though? It would certainly put their family on solid financial footing for generations to come. It would be impossible to keep it a secret if they decided to sell the coins. Would their property then be overrun with treasure hunters? What if the skeleton belonged to a Native American? How would that affect their rights to the property? What about cashing in the coins, selling the property, and letting someone else worry about it? Pull the ultimate con game on Grossbeck. Move the coins out secretly, sell him the land and the water rights, and then sell the coins. Ha! Got the last laugh on you *and* your scheming forefather(s). They all had a good laugh at that idea.

They were all exhausted. They agreed to get some rest and delay any decision.

It was not lost on any of them, least of all Mary, that she had been included in this very frank and serious discussion about the future of their *family*. They agreed to meet the next evening at the Timbers to celebrate their decision.

Lane and Steve were at the table waiting when Mary entered the Timbers. Joe had a really strange expression as he showed her to their table.

"Oh, what nice flowers," she said as she gently cupped the bouquet in her hands. She wondered why Joe had put flowers on this one table. Ernie appeared and poured wine for her and Lane and a smaller portion for Steve. She was about to rebuke Ernie and Lane. They were *all* in agreement about underage drinking. Lane interrupted her indignation.

"Mary, before we have any more discussions about the family's financial future, we need to make another very important family decision."

Mary went numb. "What do you mean?" she managed to croak. Her voice wouldn't work.

Lane took out a small velvet box, opened it up, and turned it around so Mary could see the diamond ring. "Steve and I want you to marry us." He slipped the ring on her finger.

She started blubbering like a big baby, right there in the Timbers in front of customers, with Joe and Ernie and the entire staff watching. She couldn't stop crying long enough to answer. The best she could do was bob her head up and down, holding up her new ring.

"Does that mean yes?" Lane asked, smiling through his own tears.

She composed herself just enough to sob, "Yes, yes, yes."

CUCHARA CHAPEL

It was the earliest wedding and certainly the shortest wedding ever performed in the Cuchara chapel. The few hearty guests were dressed warmly to ward off the June early-morning chill. Steve served as best man with Sampson close by, his red bandana festooned with columbines. The Reverend James Weston stood facing the congregation and the participants. When the sun's rays first touched the distant peaks, Lane nodded, and the reverend began the ceremony. After the "I dos," Lane held up a gold chain. Fastened to the chain was one of the gold coins he and Mary had brought out of the cave. Cleaned and burnished, it sparkled as the sun finally cleared the mountain and washed the chapel with morning light.

"Lane, it's gorgeous!" Mary gasped as she cradled the necklace in her hands.

"It's a wedding gift from Sven," Lane explained as he slipped it over her head.

"It's all the gold I'll ever want," she said.

"Me too," whispered Lane as he bent forward to kiss her.

Steve blushed, surprised by his parents' public intimacy. Sampson stretched mightily, his big front paws splayed out in front, his back arched and his rump stuck high in the air as he yawned with a crescendo of grunts. He plopped over on his side and looked up at Steve as if asking, "So, what's next?"

BVG